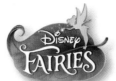

Disney Fairies

Tinker Bell

and her Magical Frie

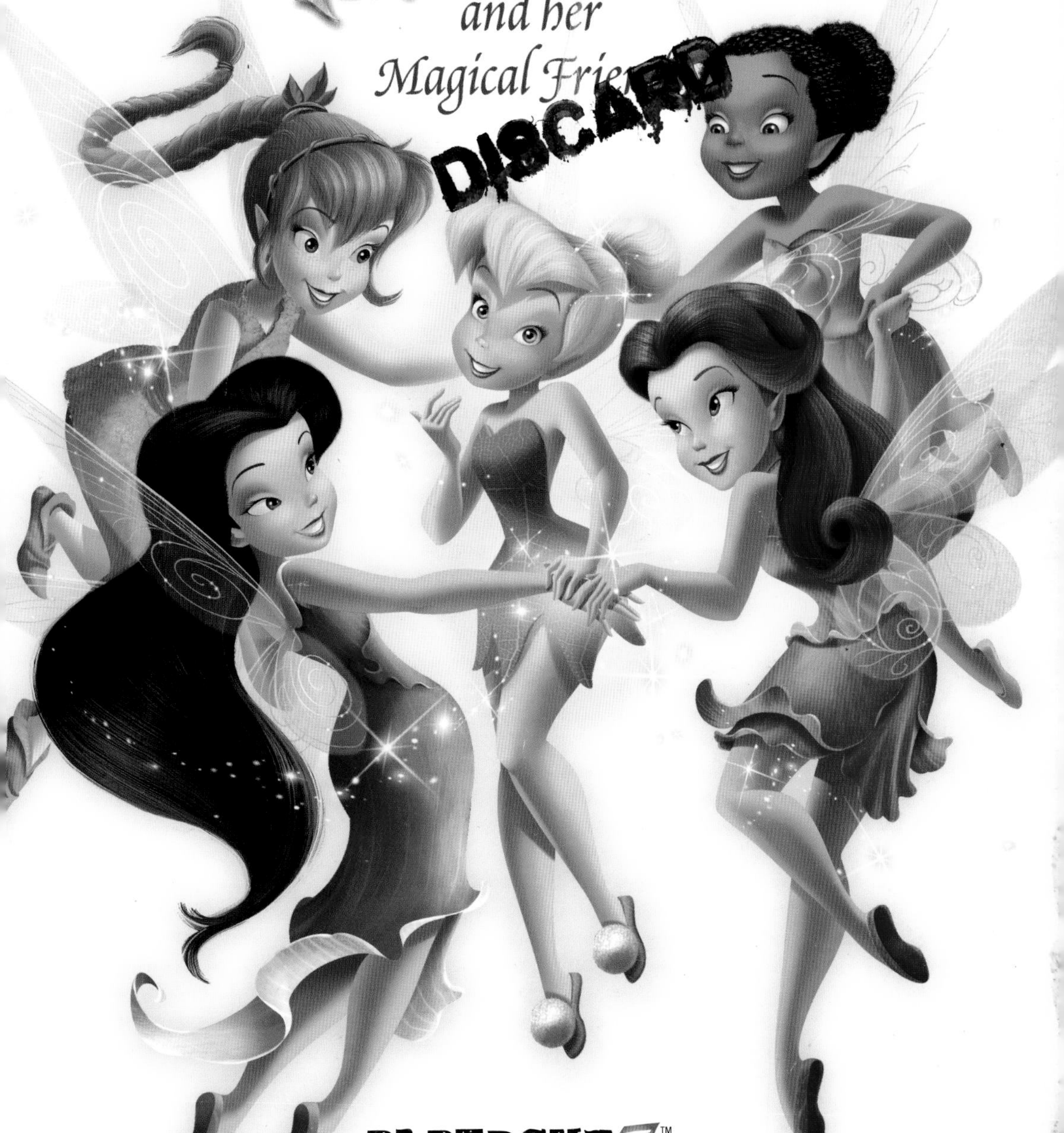

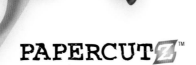

PAPERCUTZ™

Disney FAIRIES

Graphic Novels Available from
PAPERCUT Z

Graphic Novel #1
"Prilla's Talent"

Graphic Novel #2
"Tinker Bell and the
Wings of Rani"

Graphic Novel #3
"Tinker Bell and the
Day of the Dragon"

Graphic Novel #4
"Tinker Bell
to the Rescue"

Graphic Novel #5
"Tinker Bell and the
Pirate Adventure"

Graphic Novel #6
"A Present
for Tinker Bell"

Graphic Novel #7
"Tinker Bell the
Perfect Fairy"

Graphic Novel #8
"Tinker Bell and her
Stories for a Rainy Day"

Graphic Novel #9
"Tinker Bell and
her Magical Arrival"

Graphic Novel #10
"Tinker Bell and
the Lucky Rainbow"

Graphic Novel #11
"Tinker Bell and the
Most Precious Gift"

Graphic Novel #12
"Tinker Bell and the
Lost Treasure"

Graphic Novel #13
"Tinker Bell and the
Pixie Hollow Games"

Graphic Novel #14
"Tinker Bell and
Blaze"

**Tinker Bell
and the Great
Fairy Rescue**

Graphic Novel #15
"Tinker Bell and the
Secret of the Wings"

Graphic Novel #16
"Tinker Bell and the
Pirate Fairy"

Graphic Novel #1
"Tinker Bell and the
Legend of the NeverBeas

DISNEY FAIRIES graphic novels are available in paperback for $7.99 each;
in hardcover for $12.99 each except #5, $6.99PB, $10.99HC. #6-14 are $7.99PB $11.99HC.
#15 – 18 are $7.99PB $12.99HC.
Tinker Bell and the Great Fairy Rescue is $9.99 in hardcover only.
Available at booksellers everywhere.

See more at papercutz.com

Or you can order from us: Please add $4.00 for postage and handling for first book, and add $1.00 for each additional book.
Please make check payable to NBM Publishing. Send to: Papercutz, 160 Broadway, Suite 700, East Wing, New York, NY 10038
or call 800 886 1223 (9-6 EST M-F) MC-Visa-Amex accepted.

Graphic Novel #18
"Tinker Bell and her
Magical Friends"

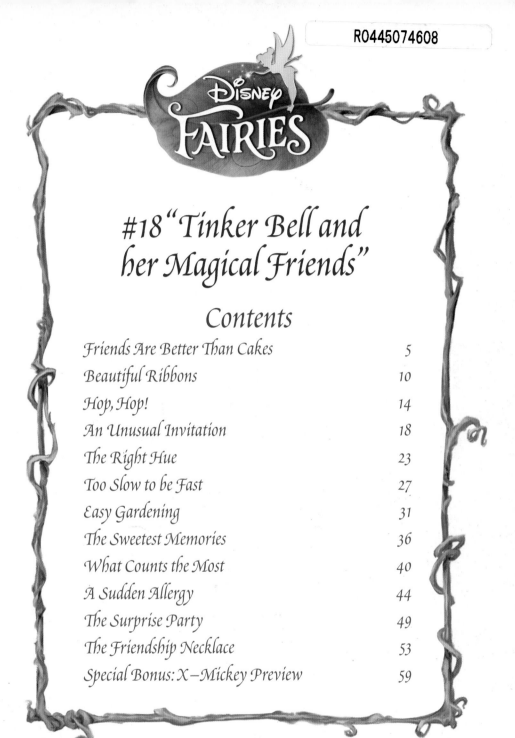

DISNEY
FAIRIES

#18 "Tinker Bell and her Magical Friends"

Contents

PAPERCUTZ™

NEW YORK

"Tinker Bell and her Magical Friends"

"Friends Are Better Than Cakes"
Script: Tea Orsi
Layout and Clean Up: Manuela Razzi
Comic Lettering: Michael Stewart
Inks: Santa Zangari
Color: Studio Kawaii

"Beautiful Ribbons"
Script: Tea Orsi
Layout: Miriam Gambino
Clean Up: Veronica Di Lorenzo
Comic Lettering: Michael Stewart
Inks: Santa Zangari
Color: Studio Kawaii

"Hop, Hop!"
Script: Tea Orsi
Layout: Giada Perissinotto
Clean Up: Veronica Di Lorenzo
Inks: Santa Zangari
Color: Studio Kawaii

"An Unusual Invitation"
Script: Tea Orsi
Pencils and inks: Monica Catalano
Color: Studio Kawaii

"The Right Hue"
Script: Carlo Panaro
Pencils: Manuela Razzi
Inks: Roberta Zanotta
Color: Studio Kawaii
Page 18 Art:
Layout, pencils, and inks:
Sara Storino
Color: Andrea Cagol

"Too Slow to be Fast"
Script: Carlo Panaro
Pencils and inks: Monica Catalano
Color: Studio Kawaii

"Easy Gardening"
Script: Tea Orsi
Layout: Emilio Urbano
Clean Up: Emanuela Razzi
Inks: Santa Zangari
Color: Studio Kawaii

"The Sweetest Memories"
Script: Tea Orsi
Layout: Giada Perissinotto
Clean Up: Veronica Di Lorenzo
Inks: Santa Zangari
Color: Studio Kawaii

"What Counts the Most"
Script: Tea Orsi
Layout: Giada Perissinotto
Clean Up: Miriam Gambino
Inks: Santa Zangari
Color: Studio Kawaii

"A Sudden Allergy"
Script:
Layout: Emilio Urbano
Clean Up: Manuela Razzi
Inks: Santa Zangari
Color: Studio Kawaii

"The Surprise Party"
Script:
Layout: Giada Perissinotto
Clean Up: Miriam Gambino
Inks: Santa Zangari
Color: Studio Kawaii

"The Friendship Necklace"
Script:
Layout: Marino Gentile
Clean Up: Veronica Di Lorenzo
Inks: Santa Zangari
Color: Studio Kawaii

Production – Dawn Guzzo
Production Coordinator – Jeff Whitman
Editor – Bethany Bryan
Jim Salicrup
Editor-in-Chief

ISBN: 978-1-62991-429-9 paperback edition
ISBN: 978-1-62991-430-5 hardcover edition
Printed in China
February 2015 by Four Color
13/F Asia One Tower
8 Fung Yip St., Chaiwan
Hong Kong

Papercutz books may be purchased for business or promotional use.
For information on bulk purchases please contact Macmillan
Corporate and Premium Sales Department at (800) 221-7945 x5442.

Distributed by Macmillan
First Papercutz Printing

"Friends are Better than Cakes"

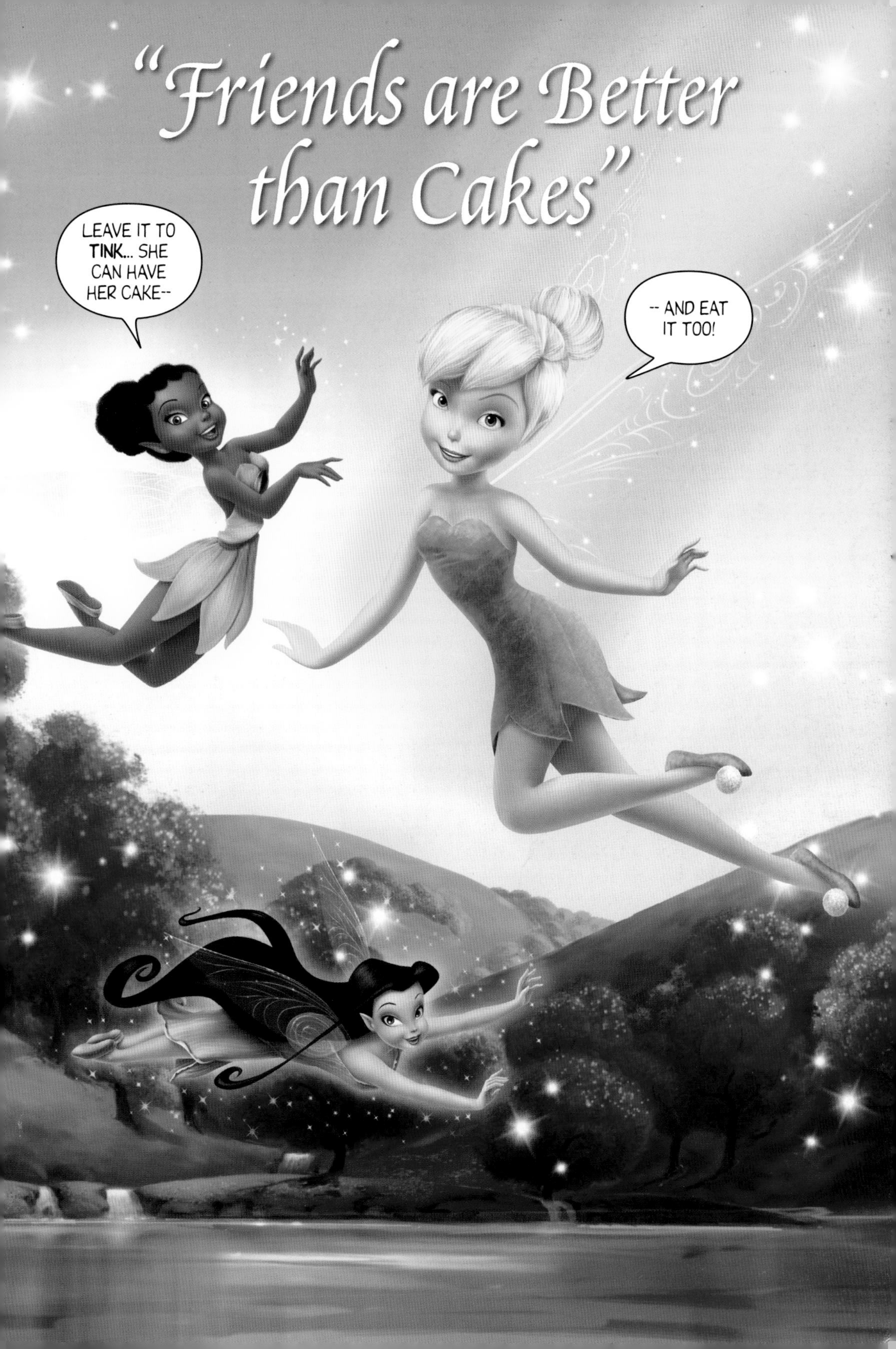

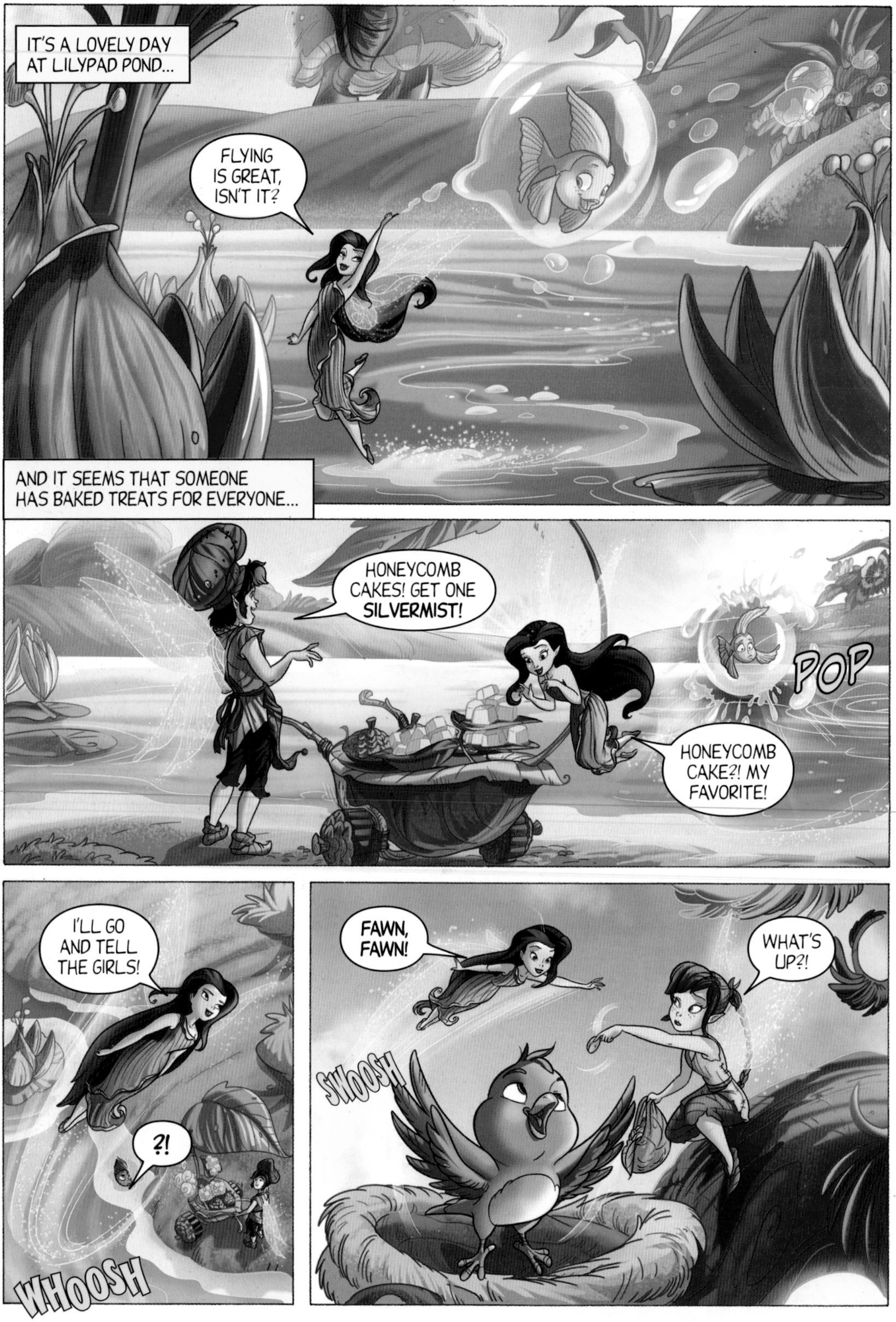
IT'S A LOVELY DAY AT LILYPAD POND...
FLYING IS GREAT, ISN'T IT?
AND IT SEEMS THAT SOMEONE HAS BAKED TREATS FOR EVERYONE...
HONEYCOMB CAKES! GET ONE SILVERMIST!
POP
HONEYCOMB CAKE?! MY FAVORITE!
I'LL GO AND TELL THE GIRLS!
?!
WHOOSH
FAWN, FAWN!
WHAT'S UP?!
SWOOSH

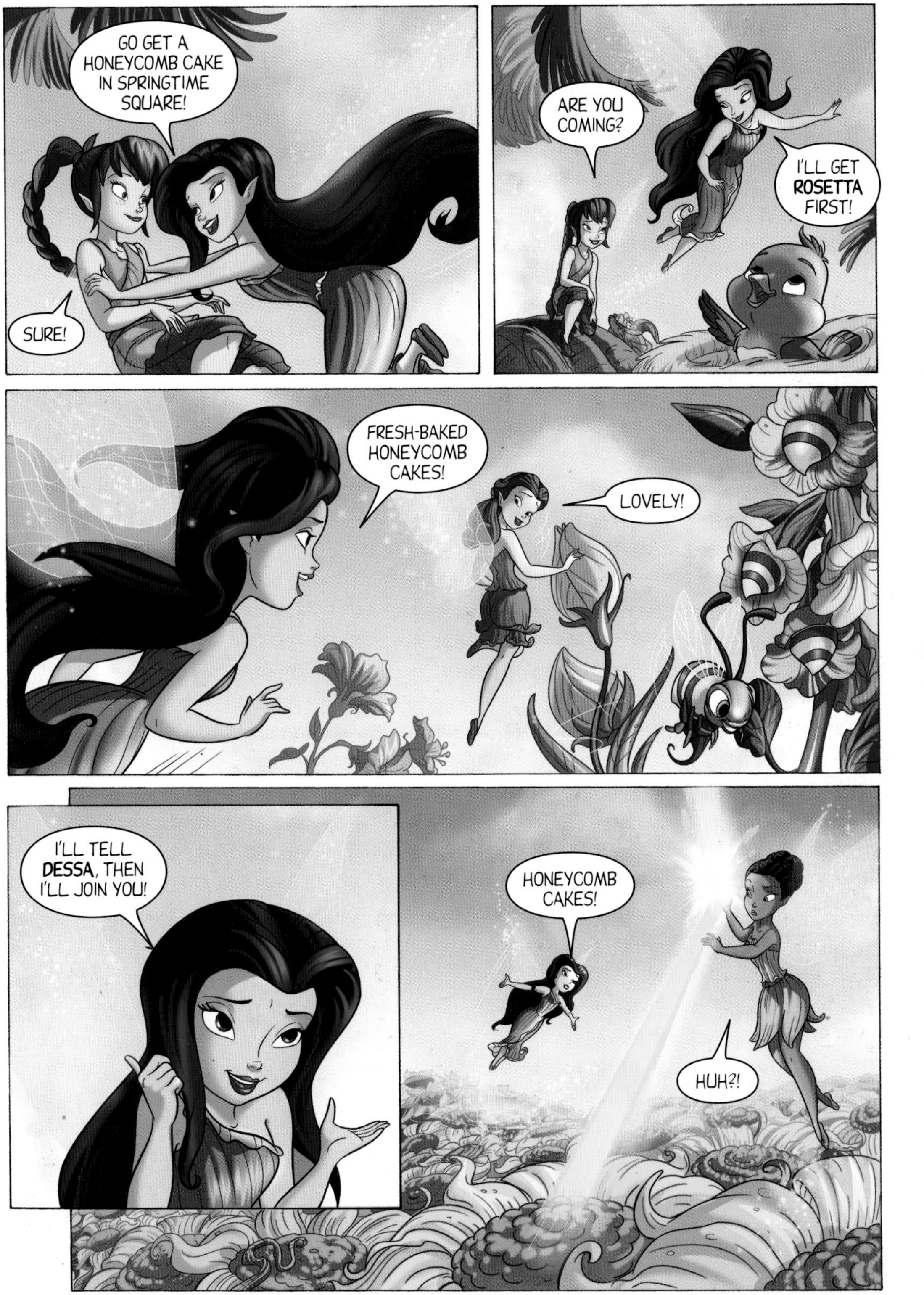
GO GET A HONEYCOMB CAKE IN SPRINGTIME SQUARE!
SURE!
ARE YOU COMING?
I'LL GET ROSETTA FIRST!
FRESH-BAKED HONEYCOMB CAKES!
LOVELY!
I'LL TELL DESSA, THEN I'LL JOIN YOU!
HONEYCOMB CAKES!
HUH?!

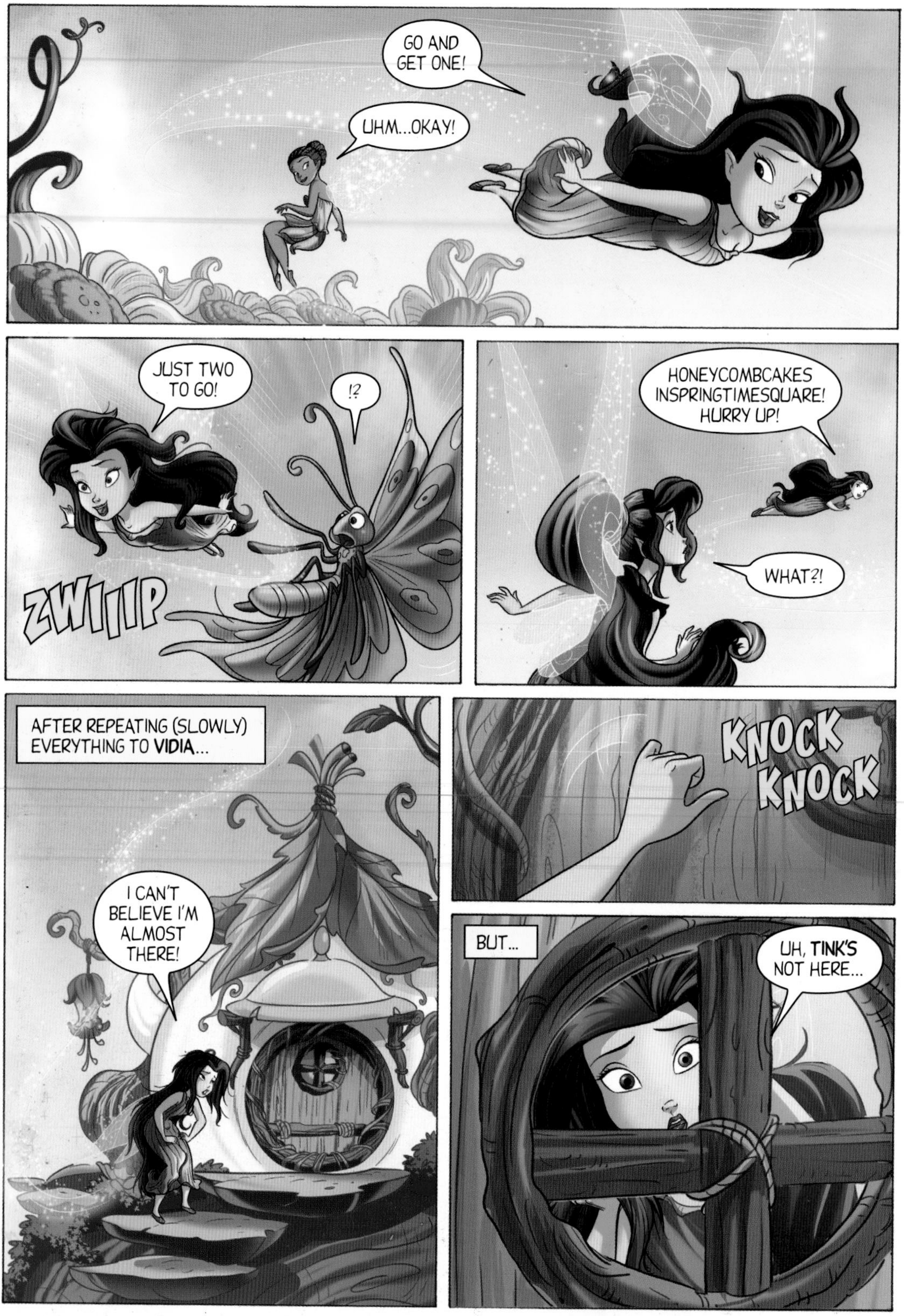
GO AND GET ONE!
UHM...OKAY!
JUST TWO TO GO!
!?
ZWIIIP
HONEYCOMBCAKES INSPRINGTIMESQUARE! HURRY UP!
WHAT?!
AFTER REPEATING (SLOWLY) EVERYTHING TO VIDIA...
I CAN'T BELIEVE I'M ALMOST THERE!
KNOCK KNOCK
BUT...
UH, TINK'S NOT HERE...

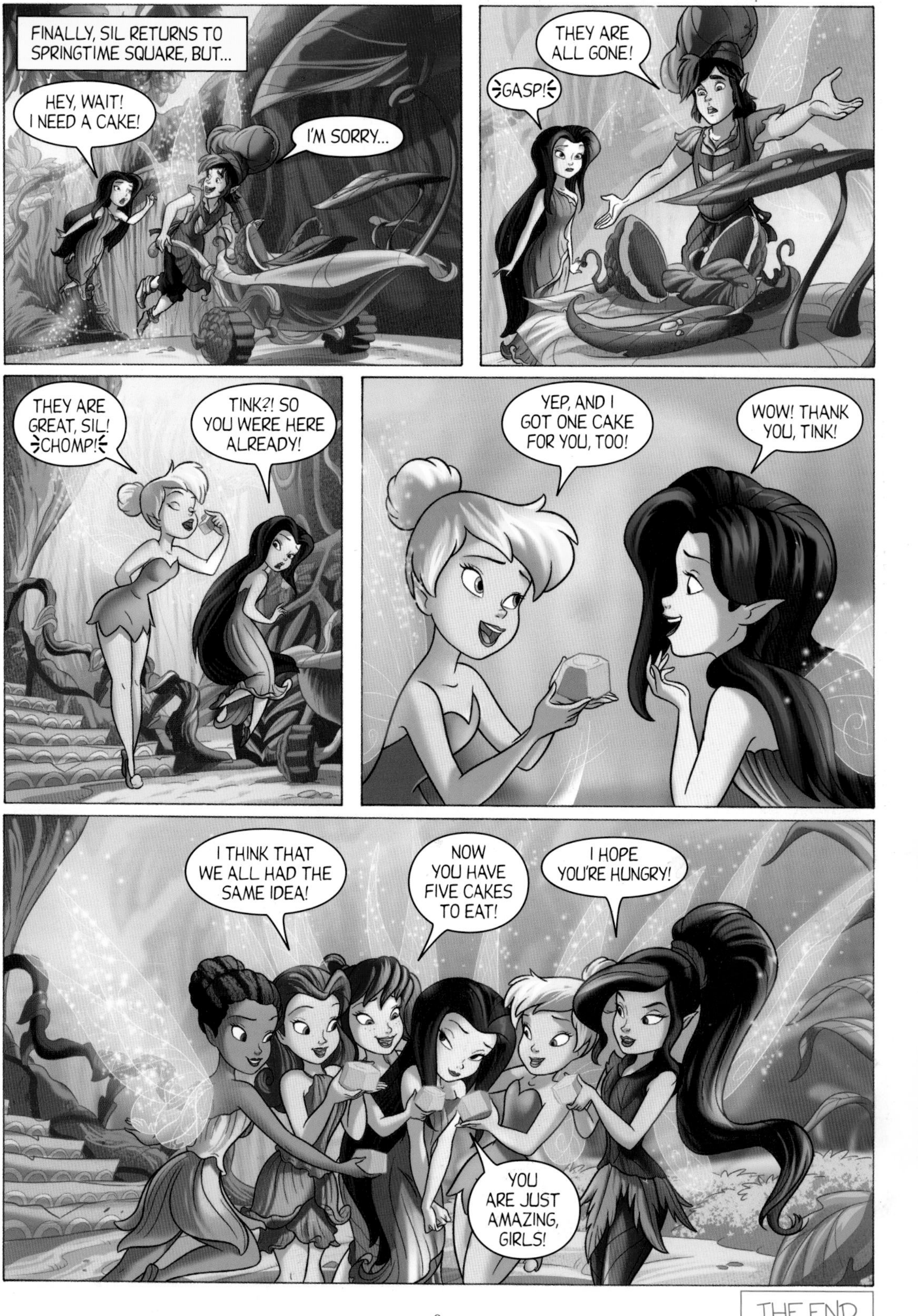

FINALLY, SIL RETURNS TO SPRINGTIME SQUARE, BUT...
HEY, WAIT! I NEED A CAKE!
I'M SORRY...
THEY ARE ALL GONE!
GASP!
THEY ARE GREAT, SIL! CHOMP!
TINK?! SO YOU WERE HERE ALREADY!
YEP, AND I GOT ONE CAKE FOR YOU, TOO!
WOW! THANK YOU, TINK!
I THINK THAT WE ALL HAD THE SAME IDEA!
NOW YOU HAVE FIVE CAKES TO EAT!
I HOPE YOU'RE HUNGRY!
YOU ARE JUST AMAZING, GIRLS!

THE END

Beautiful Ribbons

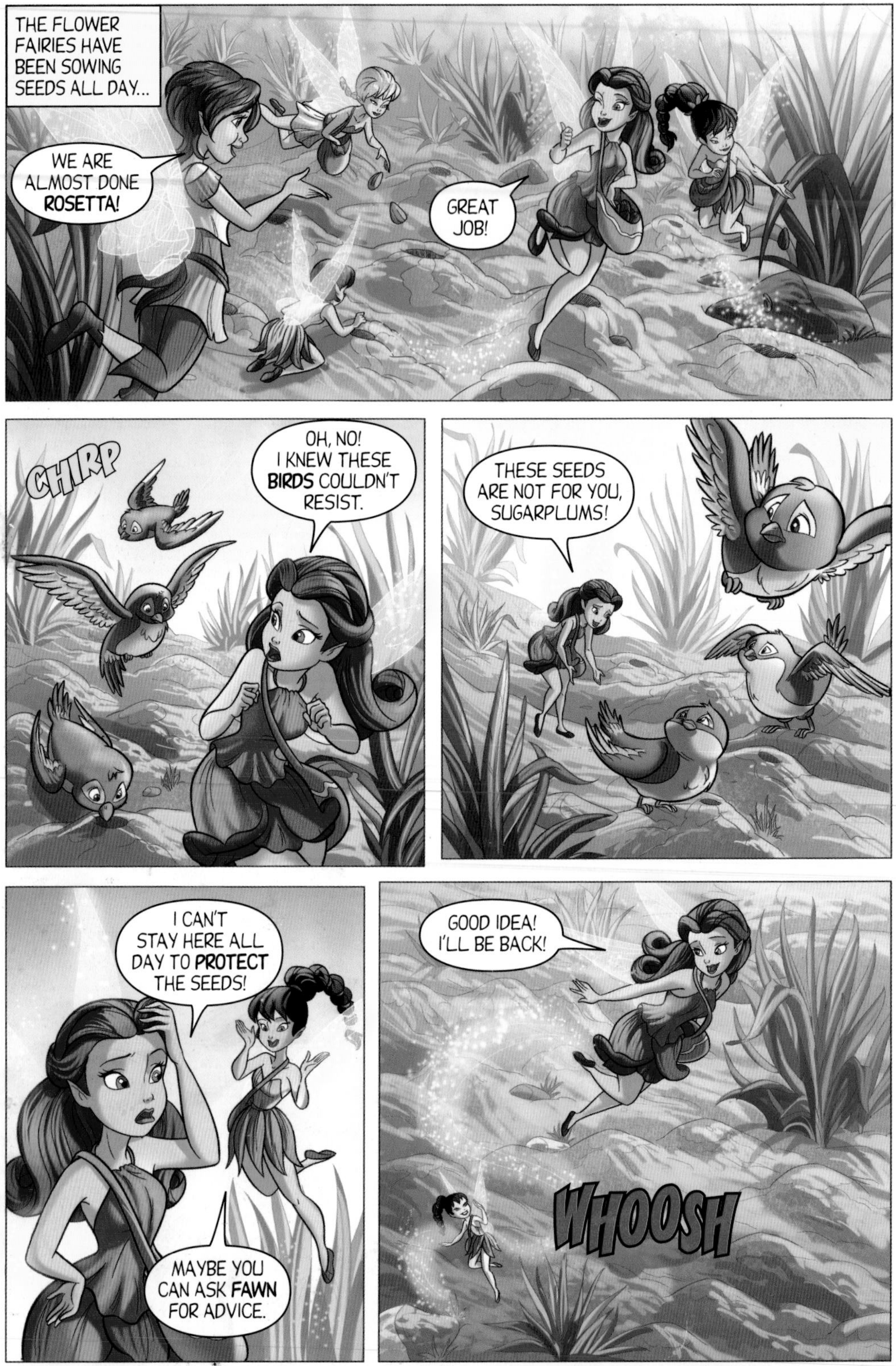

THE FLOWER FAIRIES HAVE BEEN SOWING SEEDS ALL DAY...
WE ARE ALMOST DONE ROSETTA!
GREAT JOB!
CHIRP
OH, NO! I KNEW THESE BIRDS COULDN'T RESIST.
THESE SEEDS ARE NOT FOR YOU, SUGARPLUMS!
I CAN'T STAY HERE ALL DAY TO PROTECT THE SEEDS!
MAYBE YOU CAN ASK FAWN FOR ADVICE.
GOOD IDEA! I'LL BE BACK!
WHOOSH

RO REACHES FAWN AND TELLS HER ABOUT THE PROBLEM...

YOU CAN BUILD A **PUPPET** IN THE MIDDLE OF THE FIELD.

A PUPPET?

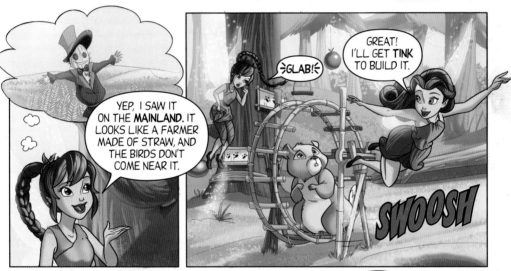

YEP, I SAW IT ON THE **MAINLAND**. IT LOOKS LIKE A FARMER MADE OF STRAW, AND THE BIRDS DON'T COME NEAR IT.

GLAB!

GREAT! I'LL GET **TINK** TO BUILD IT.

SWOOSH

NO SOONER SAID THAN DONE...

WHOA! YOU'RE AMAZING, TINK!

THANKS, WE JUST NEED TO ADD THE **FINISHING TOUCHES** NOW.

WHAT IS IT?

LET'S GO TO **THE WORKSHOP**, AND YOU'LL FIND OUT.

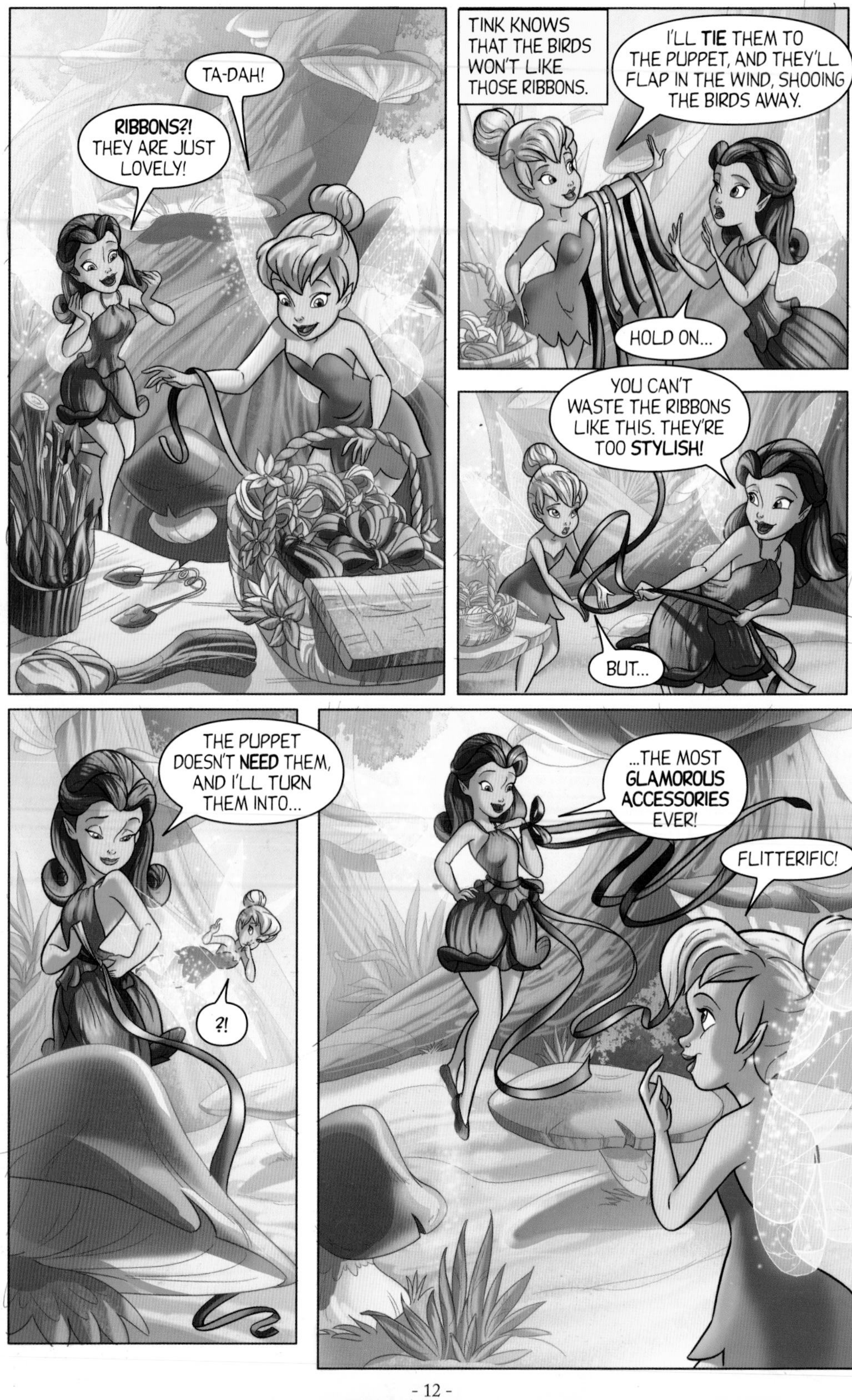
TA-DAH!
RIBBONS?! THEY ARE JUST LOVELY!
TINK KNOWS THAT THE BIRDS WON'T LIKE THOSE RIBBONS.
I'LL TIE THEM TO THE PUPPET, AND THEY'LL FLAP IN THE WIND, SHOOING THE BIRDS AWAY.
HOLD ON...
YOU CAN'T WASTE THE RIBBONS LIKE THIS. THEY'RE TOO STYLISH!
BUT...
THE PUPPET DOESN'T NEED THEM, AND I'LL TURN THEM INTO...
?!
...THE MOST GLAMOROUS ACCESSORIES EVER!
FLITTERIFIC!

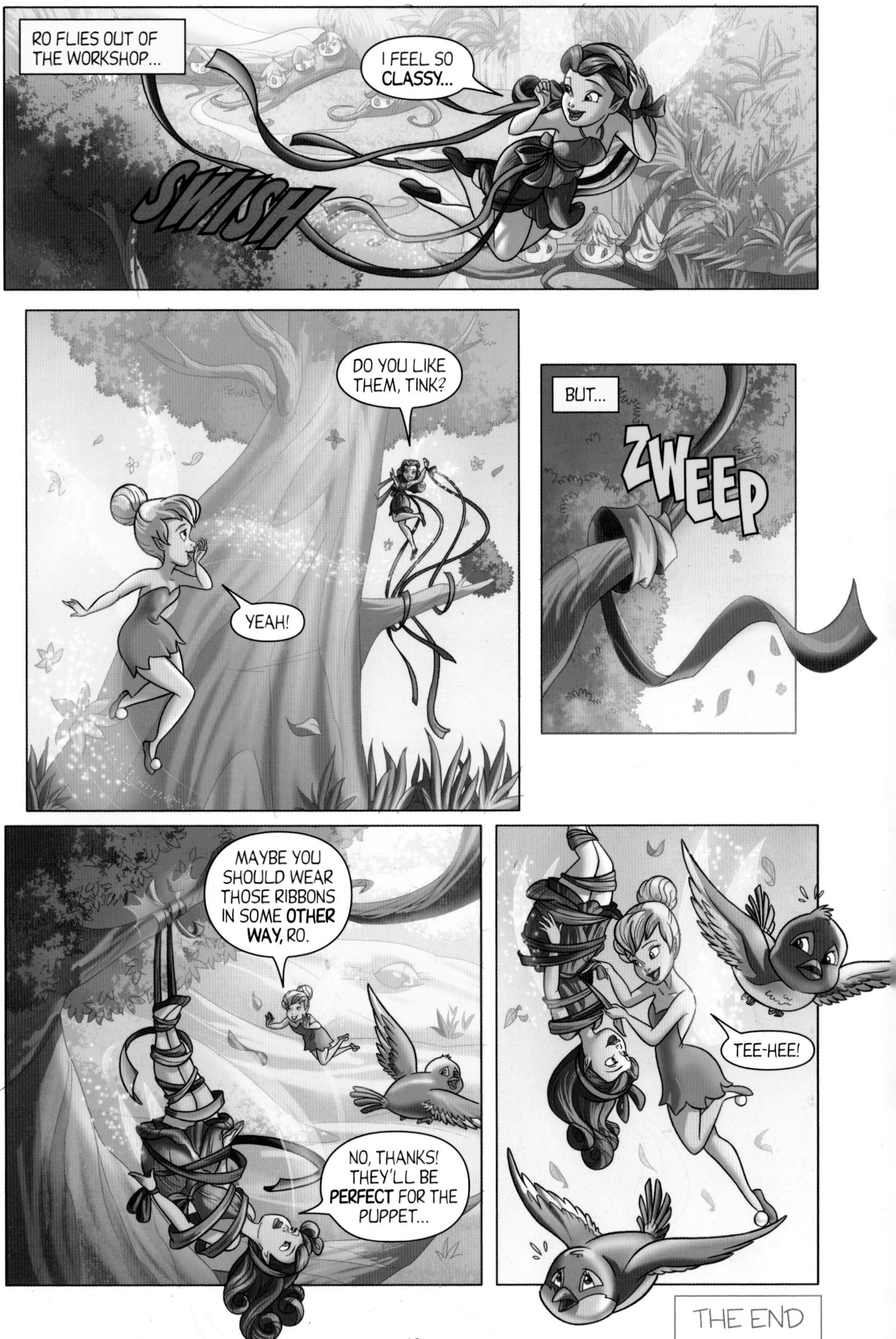
RO FLIES OUT OF THE WORKSHOP...
I FEEL SO CLASSY...
SWISH
DO YOU LIKE THEM, TINK?
YEAH!
BUT...
ZWEEP
MAYBE YOU SHOULD WEAR THOSE RIBBONS IN SOME OTHER WAY, RO.
NO, THANKS! THEY'LL BE PERFECT FOR THE PUPPET...
TEE-HEE!
THE END

Hop, Hop!

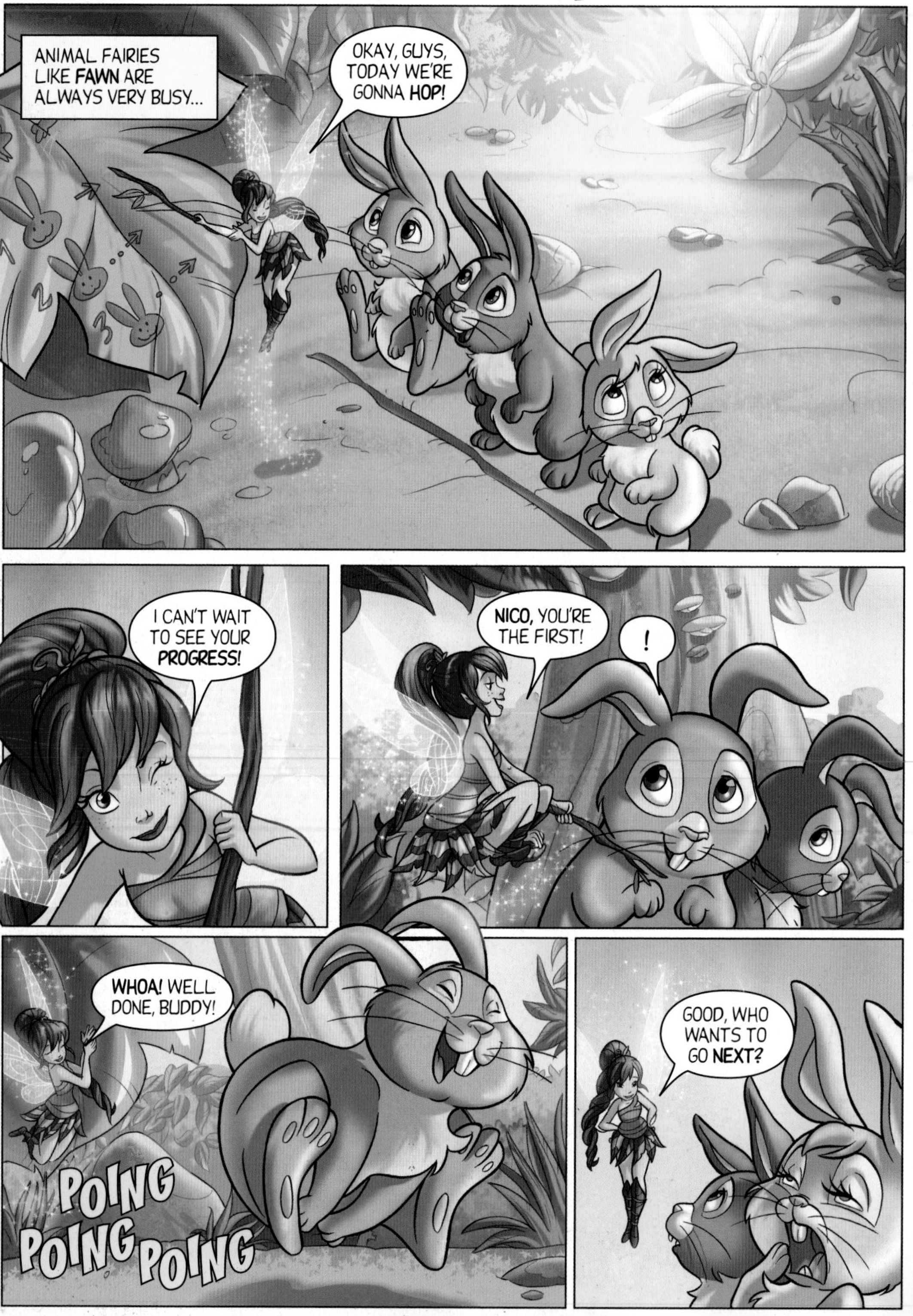
ANIMAL FAIRIES LIKE FAWN ARE ALWAYS VERY BUSY...
OKAY, GUYS, TODAY WE'RE GONNA HOP!
I CAN'T WAIT TO SEE YOUR PROGRESS!
NICO, YOU'RE THE FIRST!
!
WHOA! WELL DONE, BUDDY!
POING POING POING
GOOD, WHO WANTS TO GO NEXT?

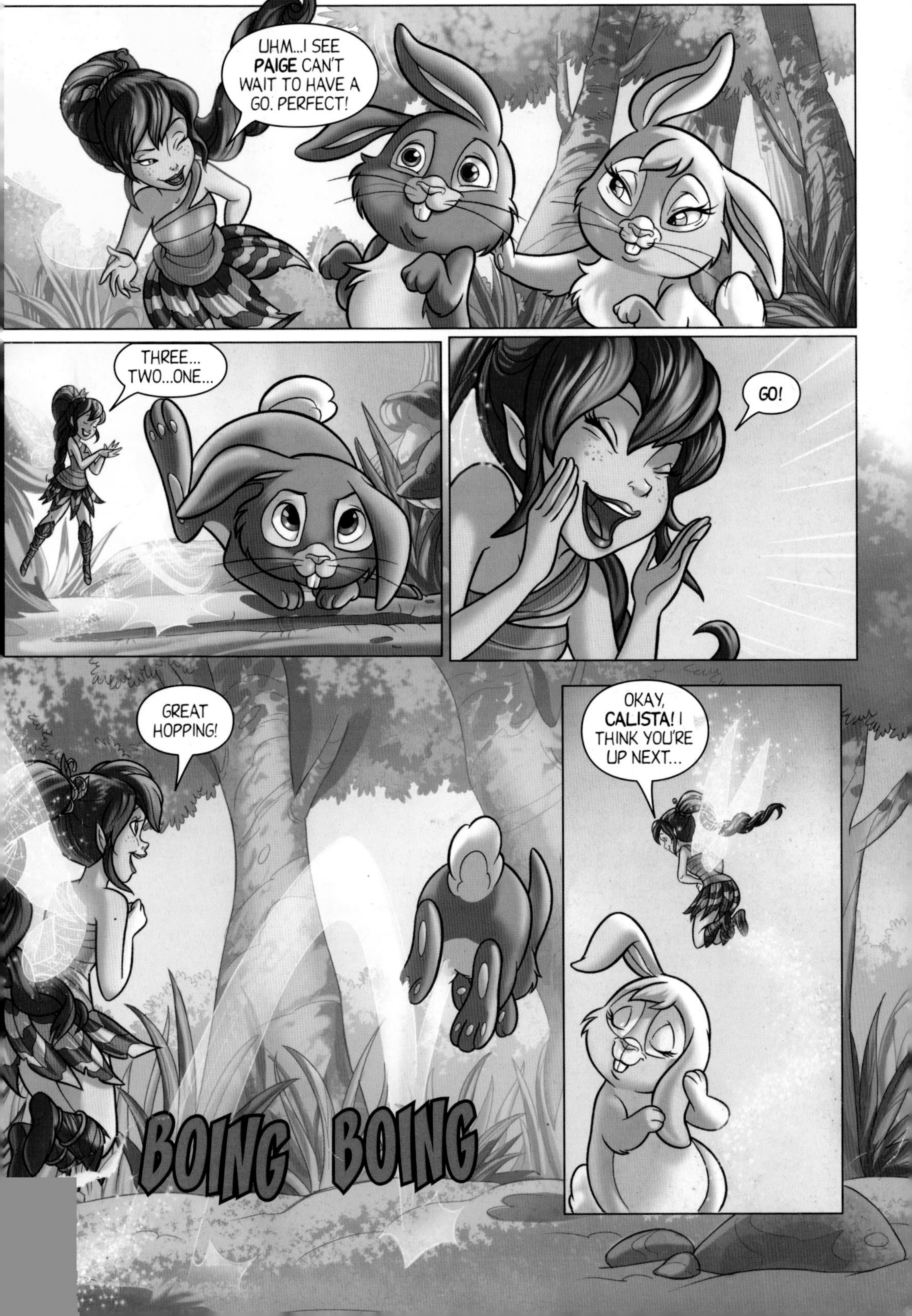
UHM...I SEE PAIGE CAN'T WAIT TO HAVE A GO. PERFECT!
THREE... TWO...ONE...
GO!
GREAT HOPPING!
BOING BOING
OKAY, CALISTA! I THINK YOU'RE UP NEXT...

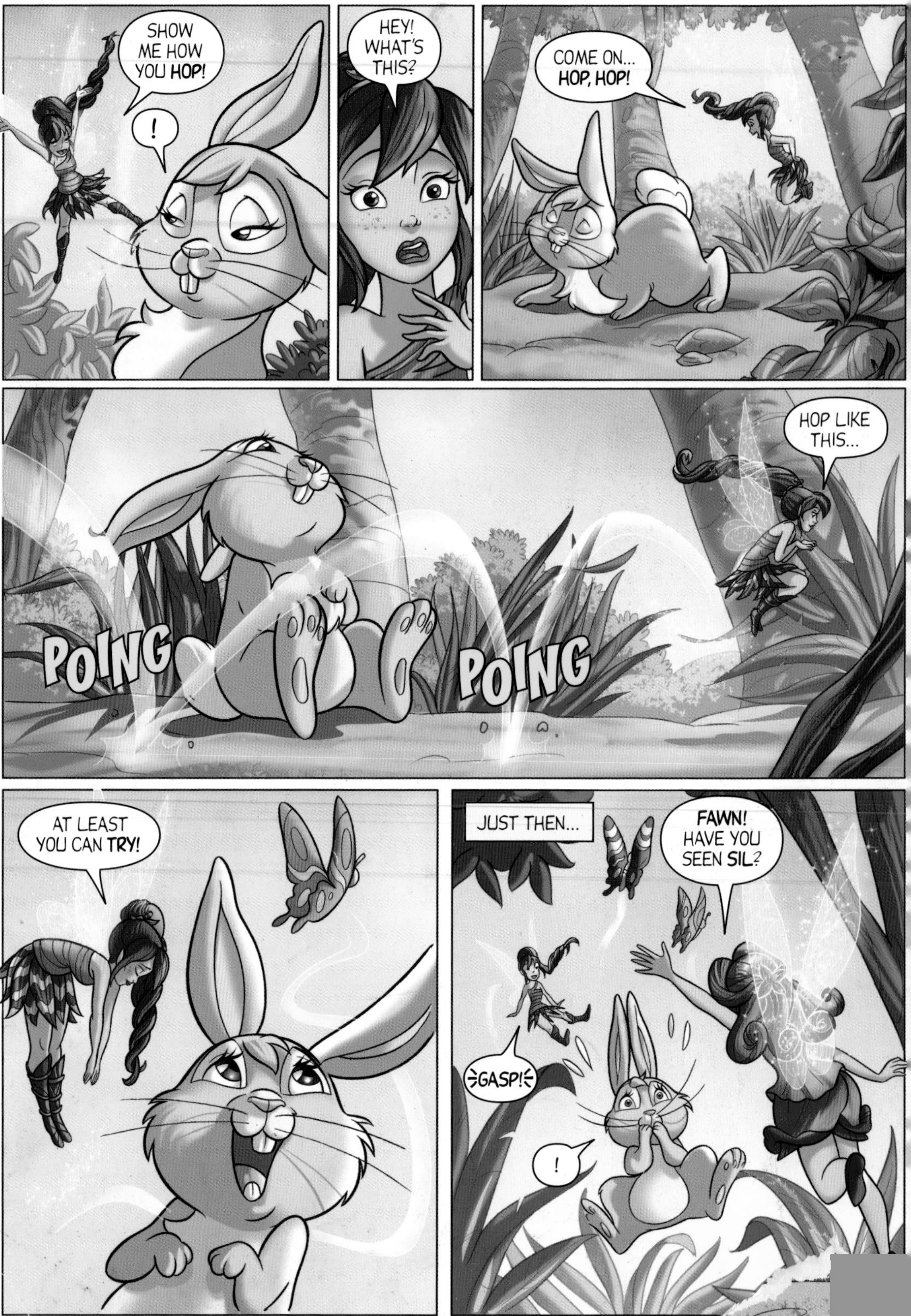
SHOW ME HOW YOU HOP!
!
HEY! WHAT'S THIS?
COME ON... HOP, HOP!
HOP LIKE THIS...
POING
POING
AT LEAST YOU CAN TRY!
JUST THEN...
FAWN! HAVE YOU SEEN SIL?
GASP!
!

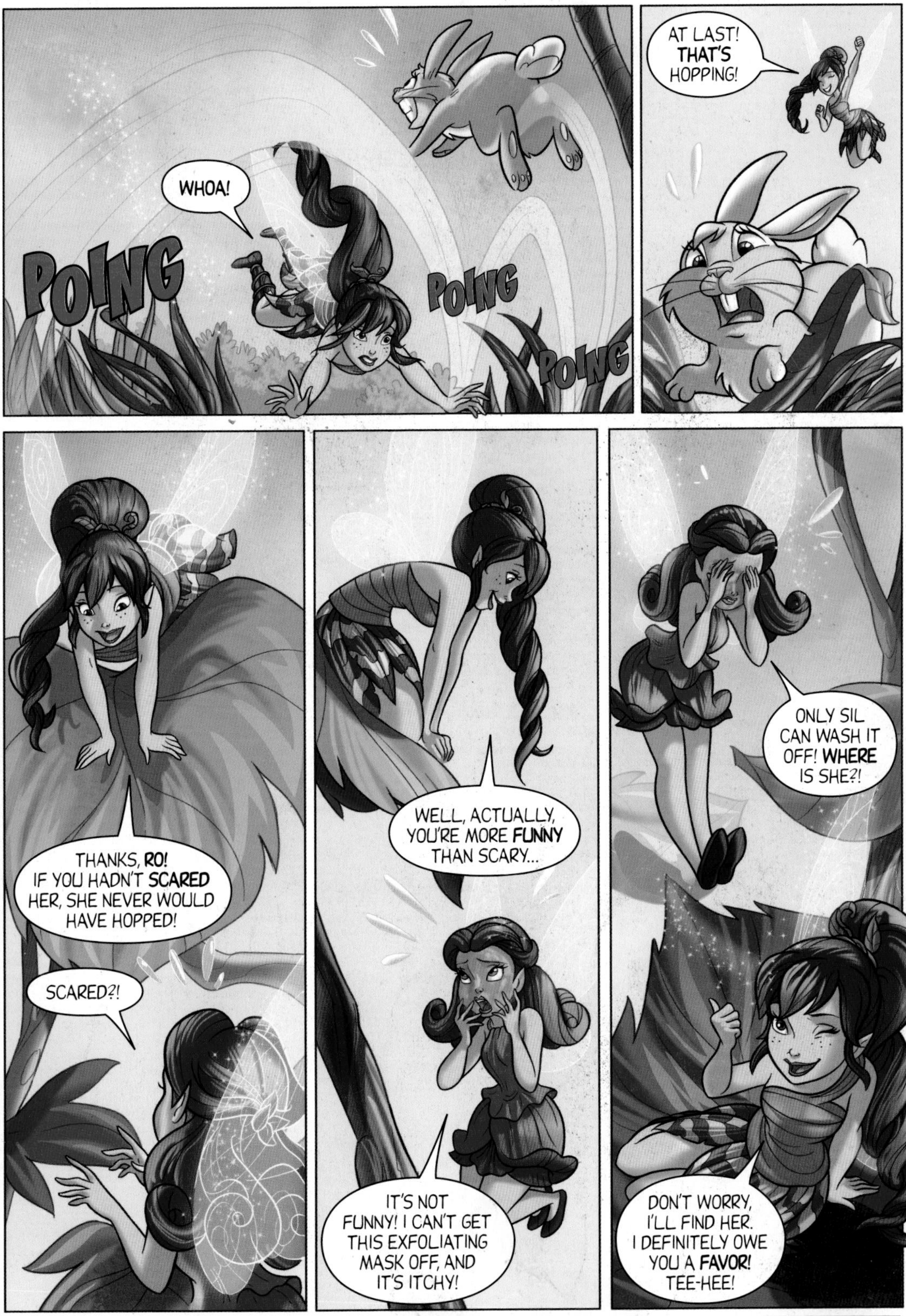
WHOA!
POING
POING
POING
AT LAST! THAT'S HOPPING!
THANKS, RO! IF YOU HADN'T SCARED HER, SHE NEVER WOULD HAVE HOPPED!
SCARED?!
WELL, ACTUALLY, YOU'RE MORE FUNNY THAN SCARY...
IT'S NOT FUNNY! I CAN'T GET THIS EXFOLIATING MASK OFF, AND IT'S ITCHY!
ONLY SIL CAN WASH IT OFF! WHERE IS SHE?!
DON'T WORRY, I'LL FIND HER. I DEFINITELY OWE YOU A FAVOR! TEE-HEE!

THE END

"An Unusual Invitation"

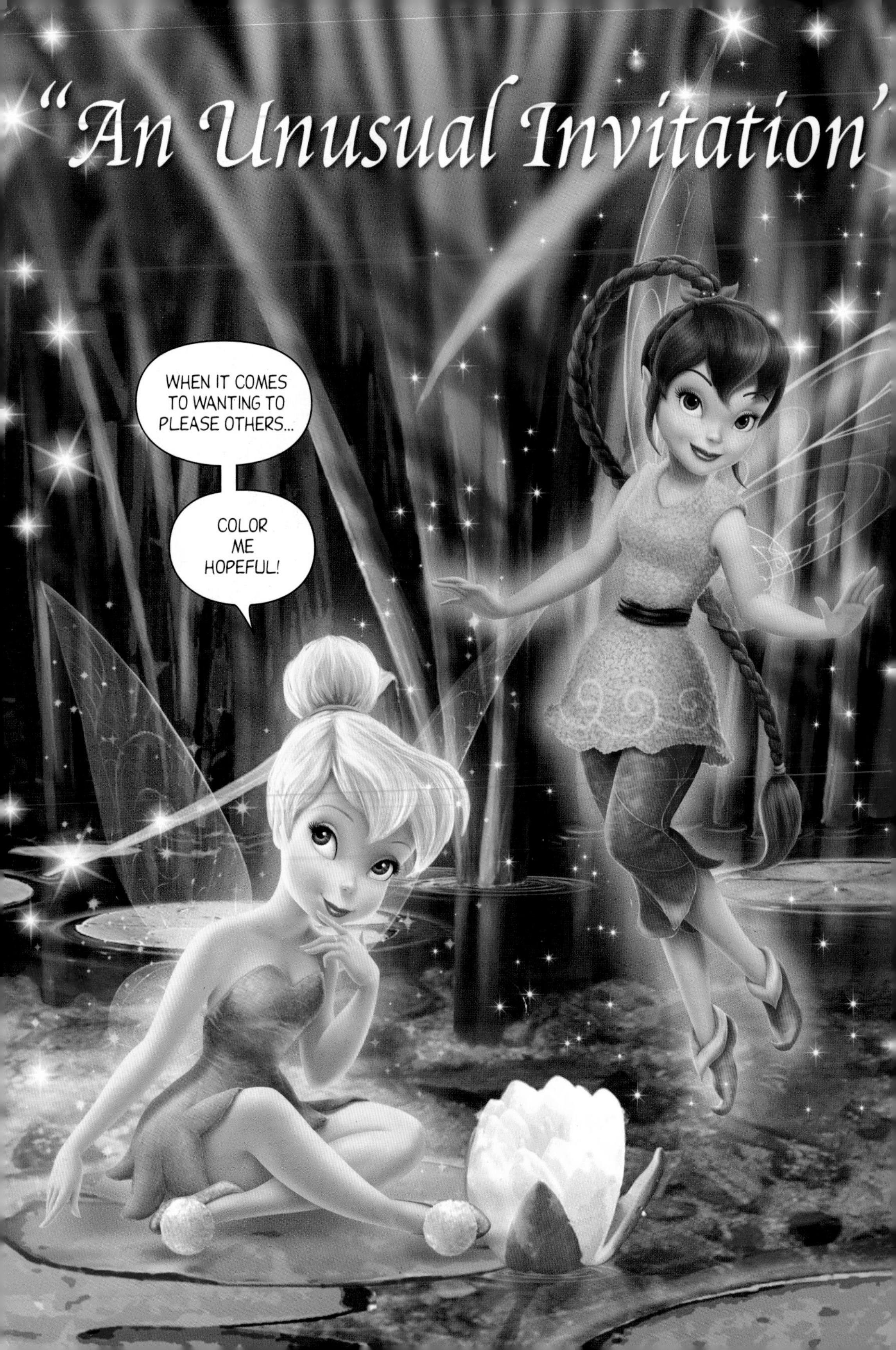
WHEN IT COMES TO WANTING TO PLEASE OTHERS...
COLOR ME HOPEFUL!

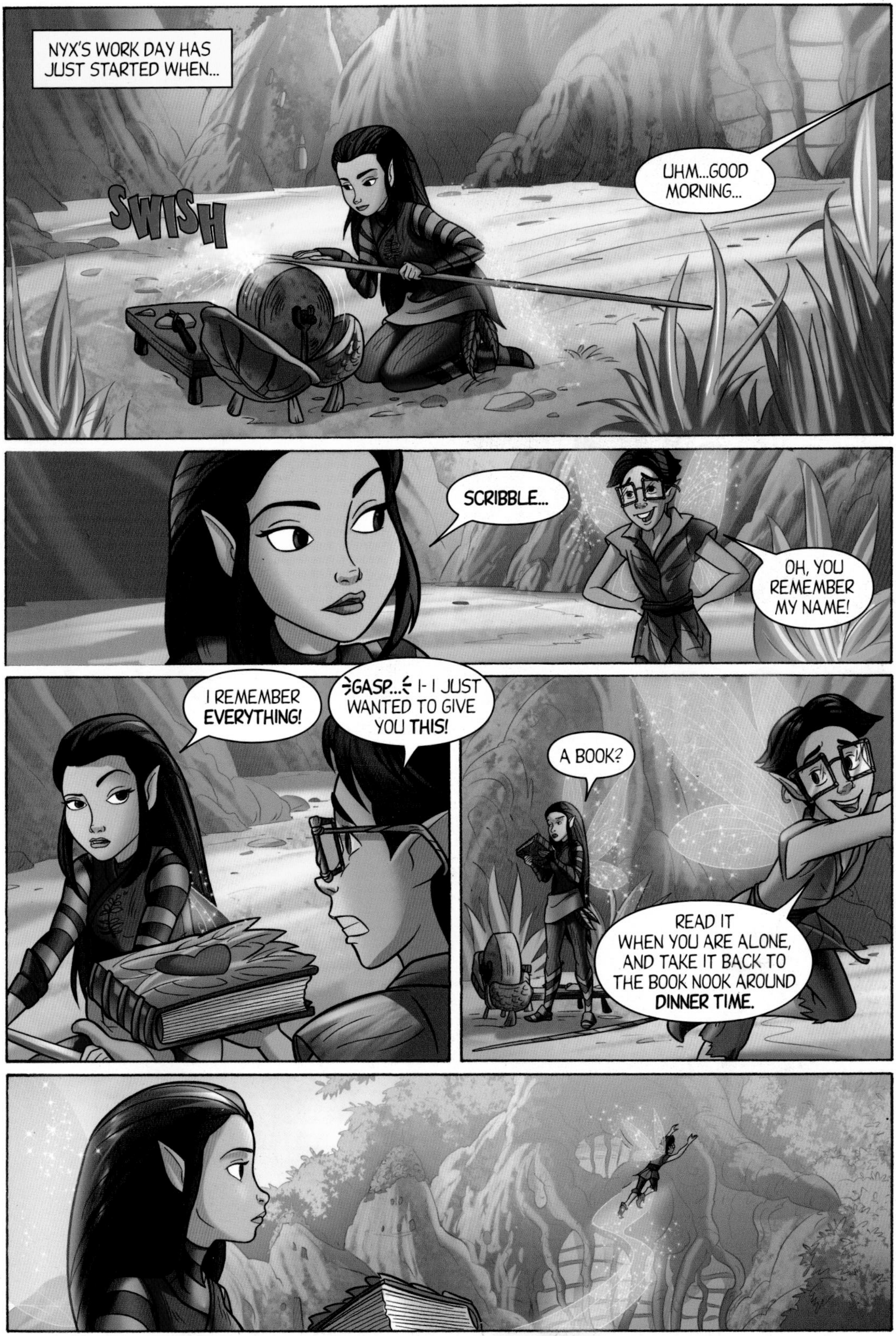
NYX'S WORK DAY HAS JUST STARTED WHEN...
SWISH
UHM...GOOD MORNING...
SCRIBBLE...
OH, YOU REMEMBER MY NAME!
I REMEMBER EVERYTHING!
GASP... I- I JUST WANTED TO GIVE YOU THIS!
A BOOK?
READ IT WHEN YOU ARE ALONE, AND TAKE IT BACK TO THE BOOK NOOK AROUND DINNER TIME.

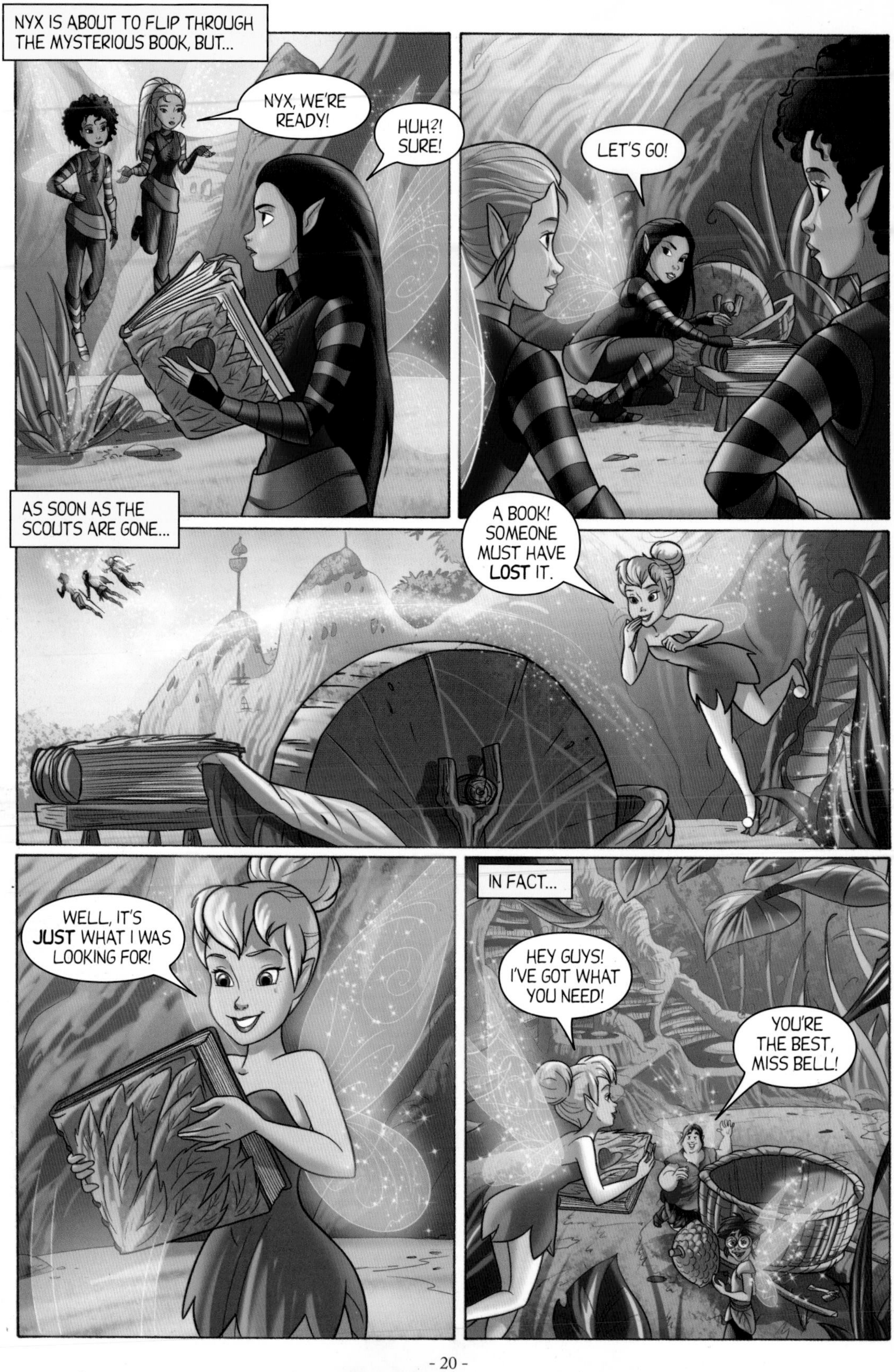

NYX IS ABOUT TO FLIP THROUGH THE MYSTERIOUS BOOK, BUT...
NYX, WE'RE READY!
HUH?! SURE!
LET'S GO!
AS SOON AS THE SCOUTS ARE GONE...
A BOOK! SOMEONE MUST HAVE **LOST** IT.
WELL, IT'S **JUST** WHAT I WAS LOOKING FOR!
IN FACT...
HEY GUYS! I'VE GOT WHAT YOU NEED!
YOU'RE THE BEST, MISS BELL!

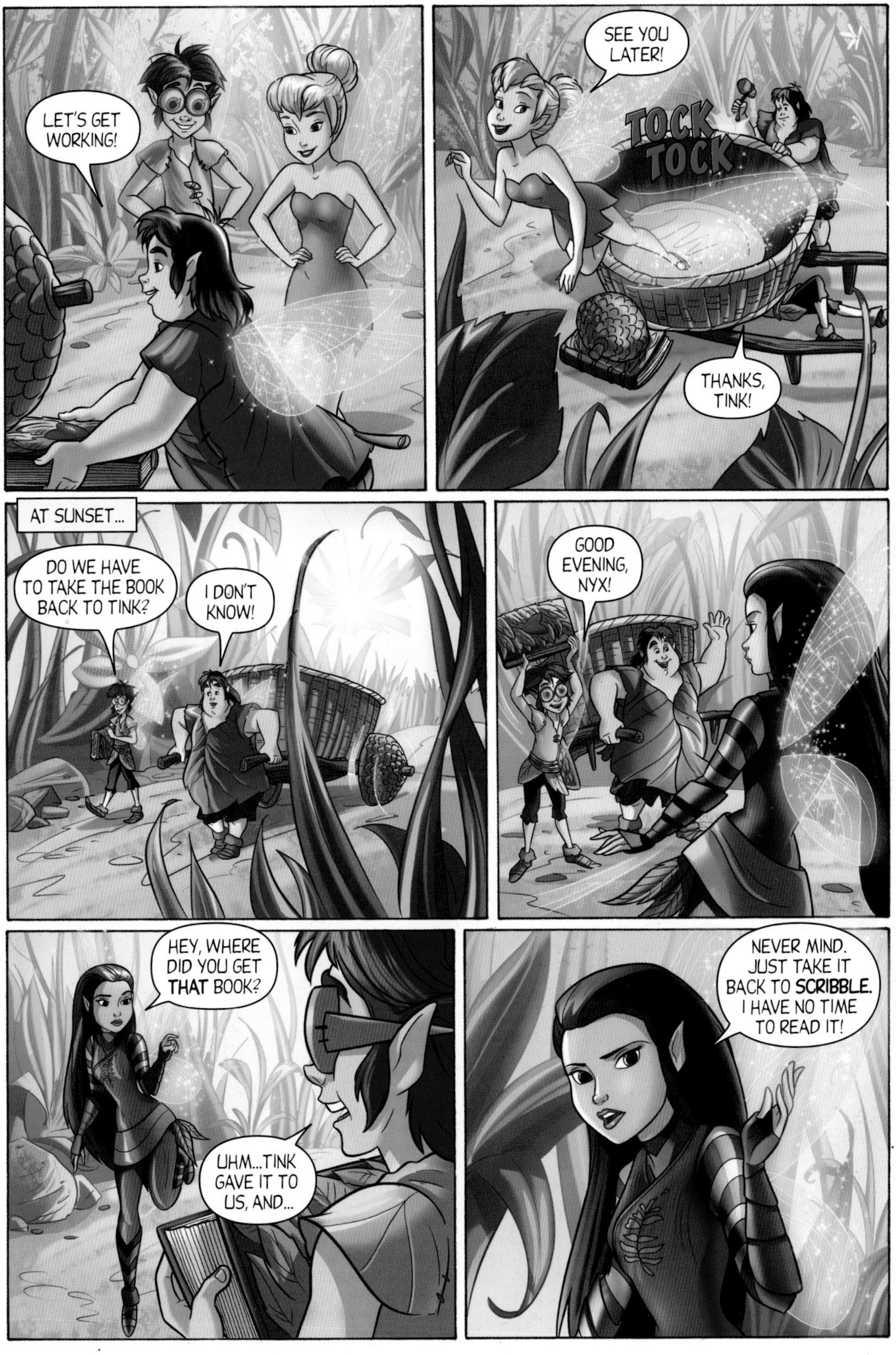
LET'S GET WORKING!
SEE YOU LATER!
TOCK TOCK
THANKS, TINK!
AT SUNSET...
DO WE HAVE TO TAKE THE BOOK BACK TO TINK?
I DON'T KNOW!
GOOD EVENING, NYX!
HEY, WHERE DID YOU GET THAT BOOK?
UHM...TINK GAVE IT TO US, AND...
NEVER MIND. JUST TAKE IT BACK TO SCRIBBLE. I HAVE NO TIME TO READ IT!

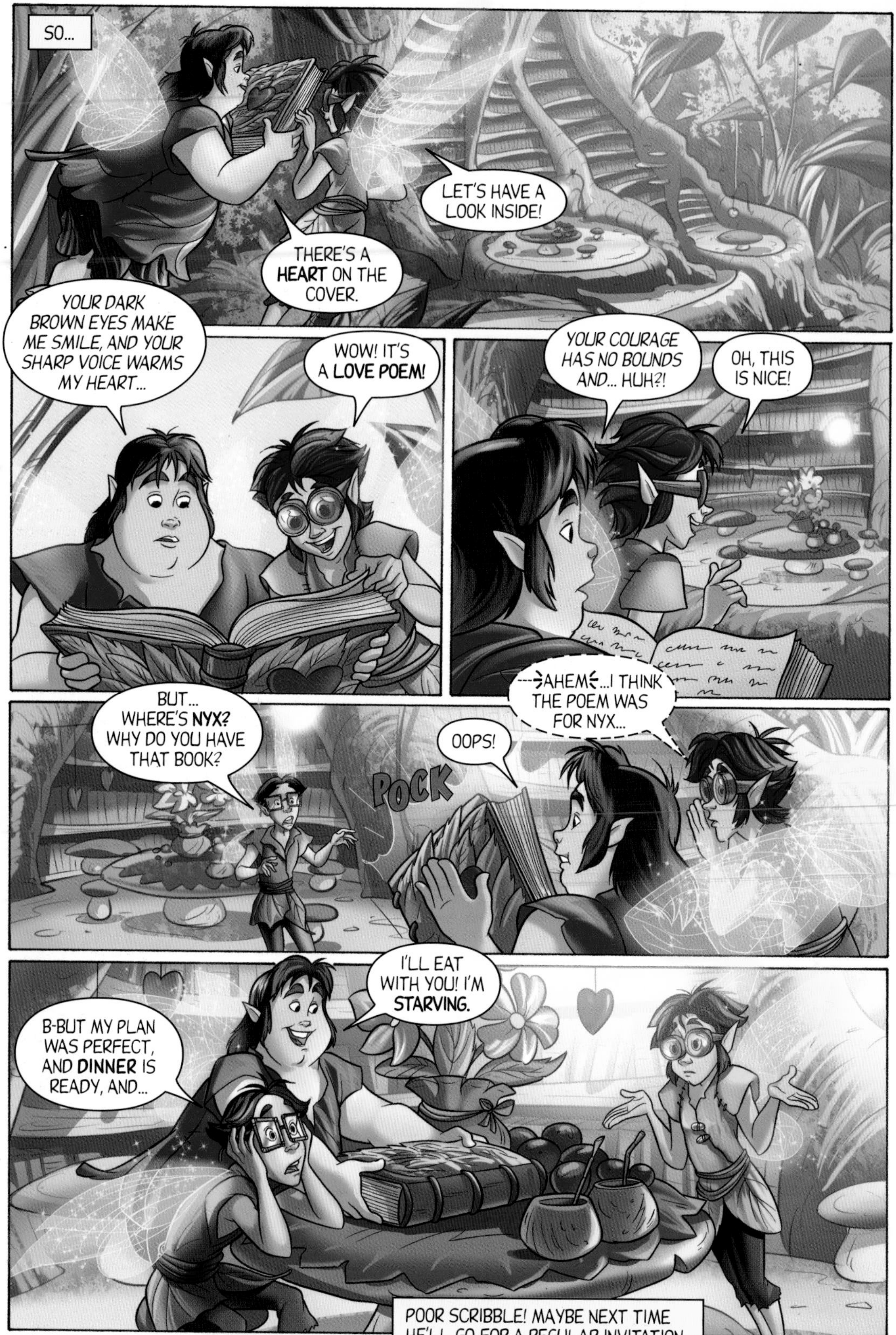
SO...
THERE'S A HEART ON THE COVER.
LET'S HAVE A LOOK INSIDE!
YOUR DARK BROWN EYES MAKE ME SMILE, AND YOUR SHARP VOICE WARMS MY HEART...
WOW! IT'S A LOVE POEM!
YOUR COURAGE HAS NO BOUNDS AND... HUH?!
OH, THIS IS NICE!
BUT... WHERE'S NYX? WHY DO YOU HAVE THAT BOOK?
POCK
OOPS!
---AHEM...I THINK THE POEM WAS FOR NYX...
B-BUT MY PLAN WAS PERFECT, AND DINNER IS READY, AND...
I'LL EAT WITH YOU! I'M STARVING.
POOR SCRIBBLE! MAYBE NEXT TIME HE'LL GO FOR A REGULAR INVITATION.

THE END

The Right Hue

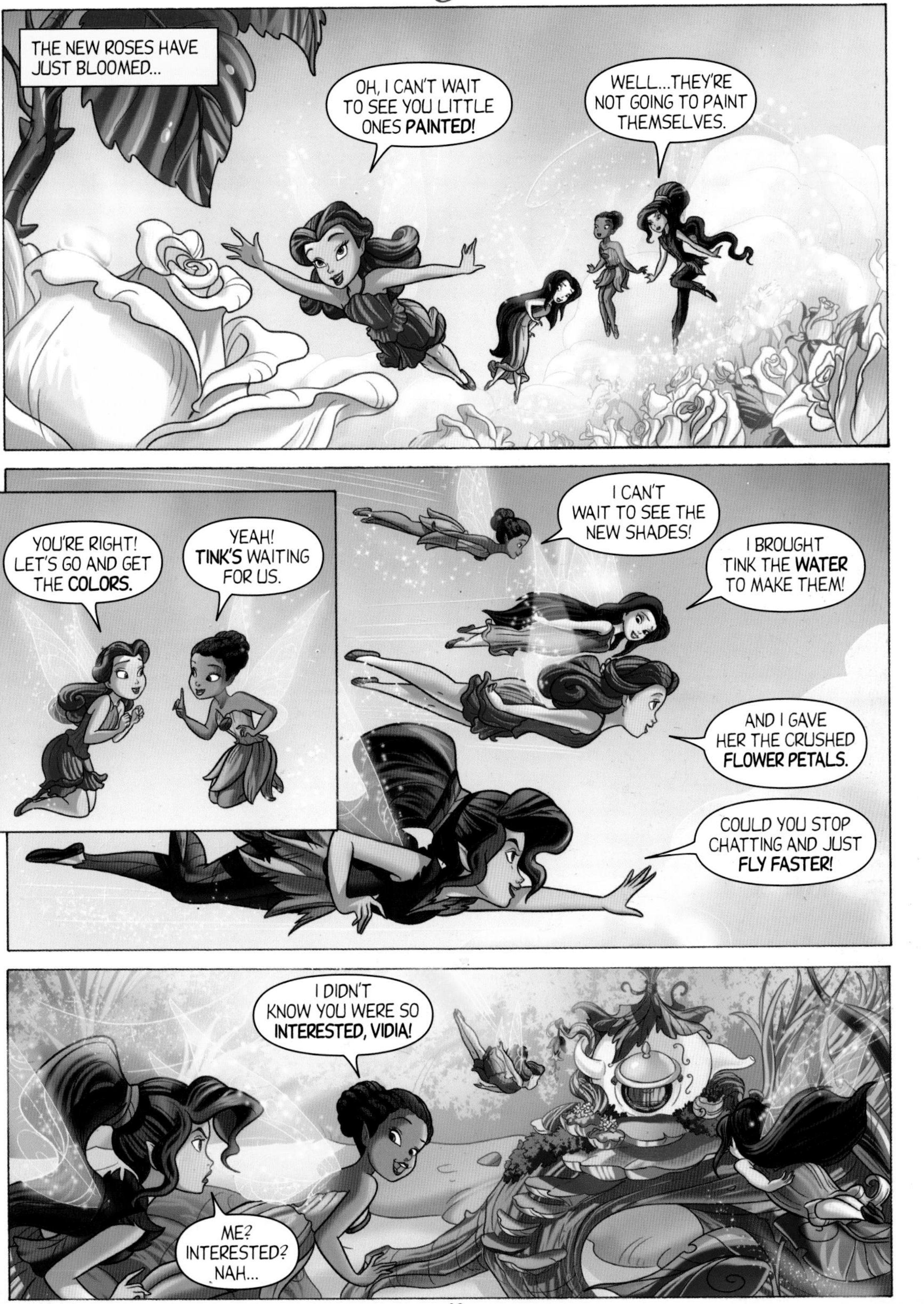

THE NEW ROSES HAVE JUST BLOOMED...
OH, I CAN'T WAIT TO SEE YOU LITTLE ONES **PAINTED!**
WELL...THEY'RE NOT GOING TO PAINT THEMSELVES.
YOU'RE RIGHT! LET'S GO AND GET THE **COLORS.**
YEAH! **TINK'S** WAITING FOR US.
I CAN'T WAIT TO SEE THE NEW SHADES!
I BROUGHT TINK THE **WATER** TO MAKE THEM!
AND I GAVE HER THE CRUSHED **FLOWER PETALS.**
COULD YOU STOP CHATTING AND JUST **FLY FASTER!**
I DIDN'T KNOW YOU WERE SO **INTERESTED, VIDIA!**
ME? INTERESTED? NAH...

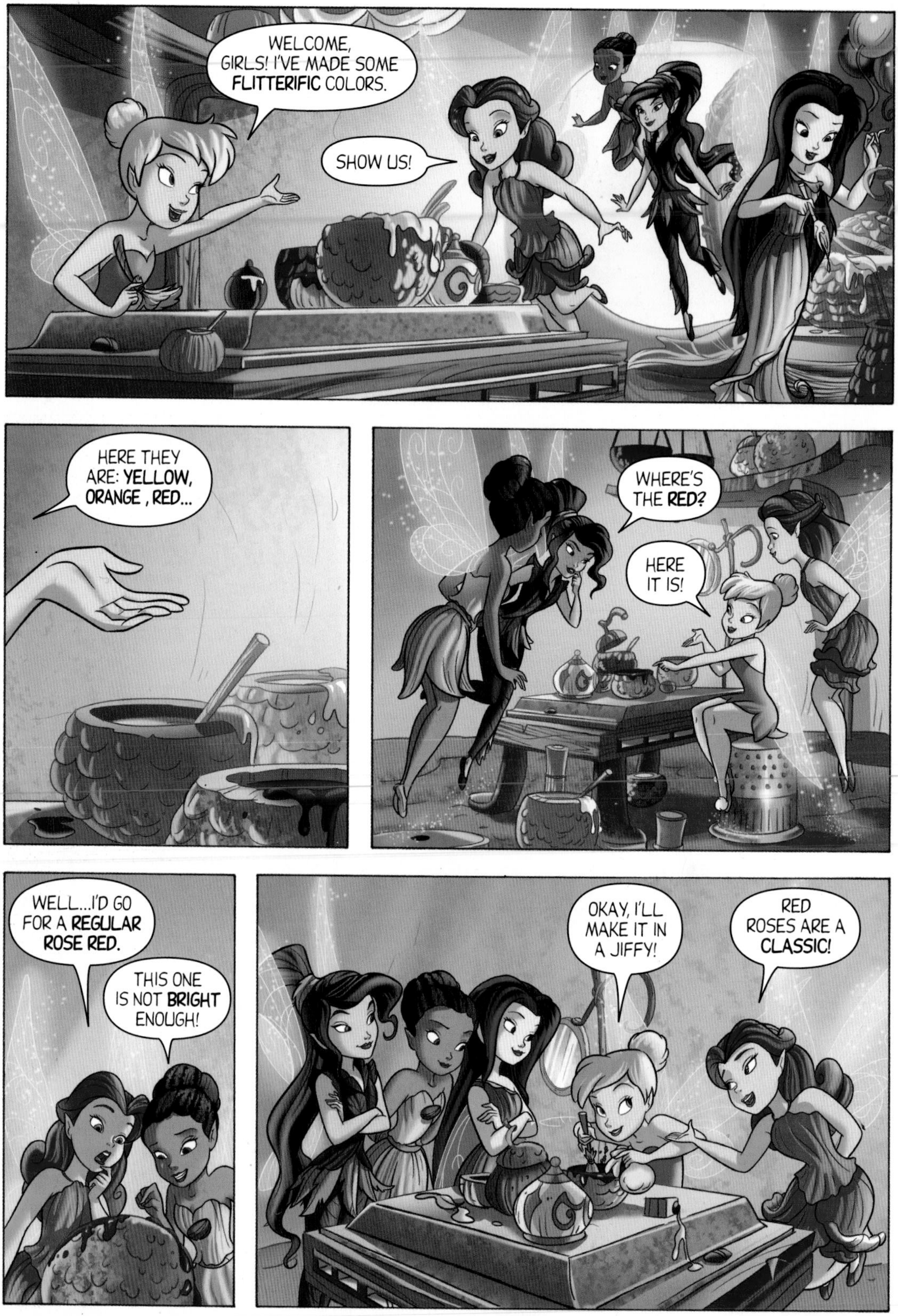
WELCOME, GIRLS! I'VE MADE SOME **FLITTERIFIC** COLORS.
SHOW US!
HERE THEY ARE: **YELLOW, ORANGE , RED...**
WHERE'S THE **RED?**
HERE IT IS!
WELL...I'D GO FOR A **REGULAR ROSE RED.**
THIS ONE IS NOT **BRIGHT** ENOUGH!
OKAY, I'LL MAKE IT IN A JIFFY!
RED ROSES ARE A **CLASSIC!**

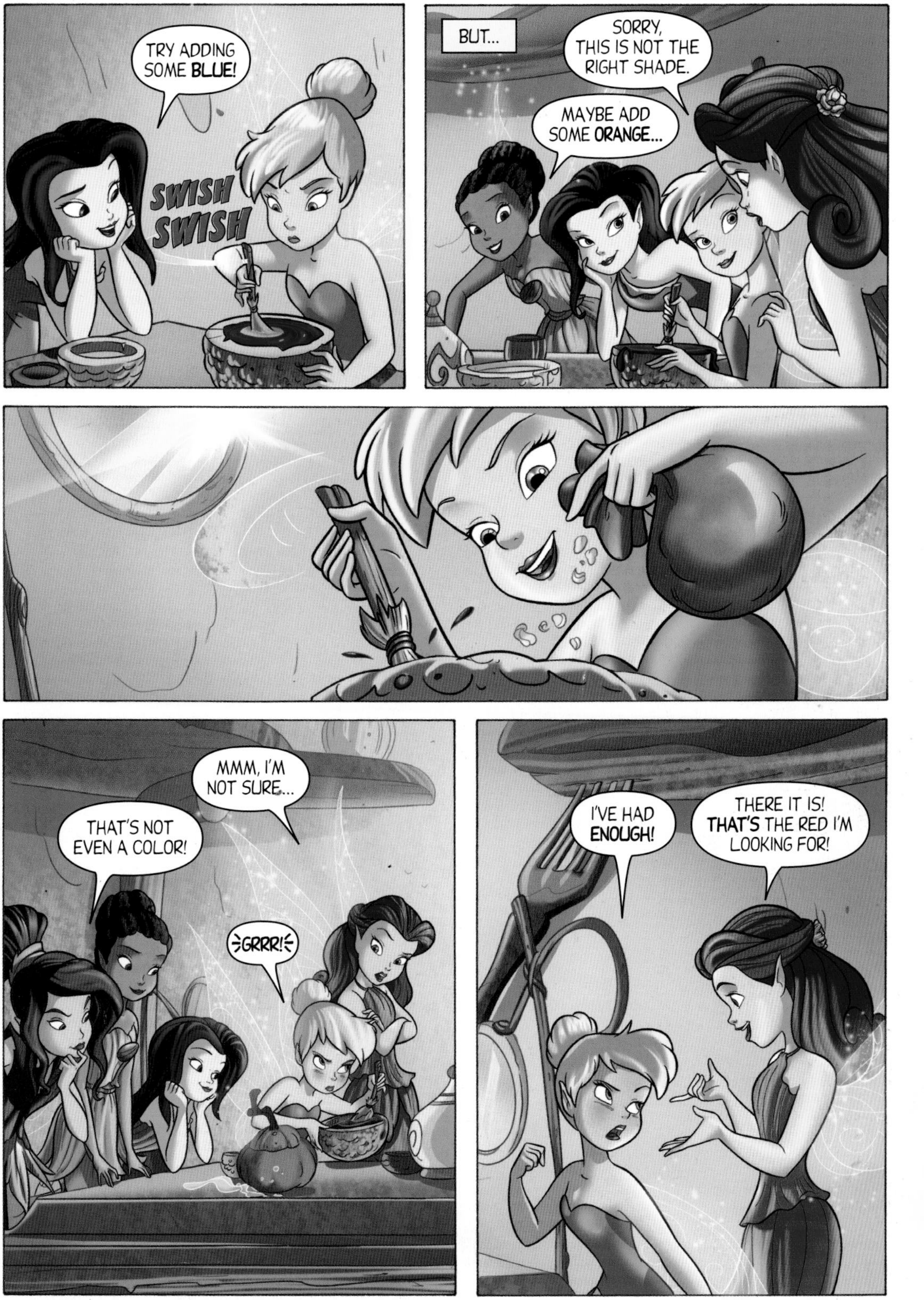
TRY ADDING SOME BLUE!
SWISH SWISH
BUT...
SORRY, THIS IS NOT THE RIGHT SHADE.
MAYBE ADD SOME ORANGE...
MMM, I'M NOT SURE...
THAT'S NOT EVEN A COLOR!
GRRR!
I'VE HAD ENOUGH!
THERE IT IS! THAT'S THE RED I'M LOOKING FOR!

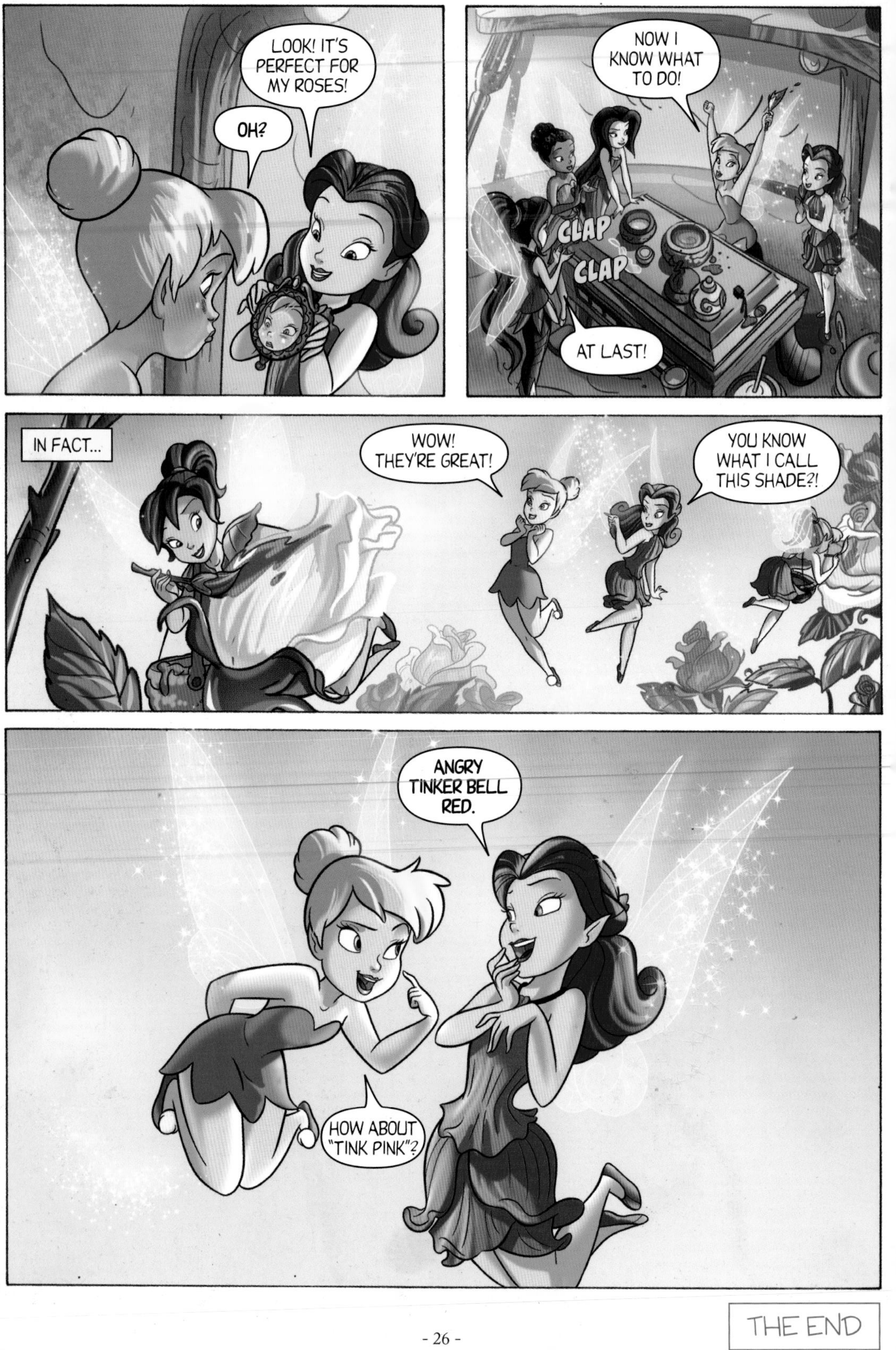
LOOK! IT'S PERFECT FOR MY ROSES!
OH?
NOW I KNOW WHAT TO DO!
CLAP
CLAP
AT LAST!
IN FACT...
WOW! THEY'RE GREAT!
YOU KNOW WHAT I CALL THIS SHADE?!
ANGRY TINKER BELL RED.
HOW ABOUT "TINK PINK"?

THE END

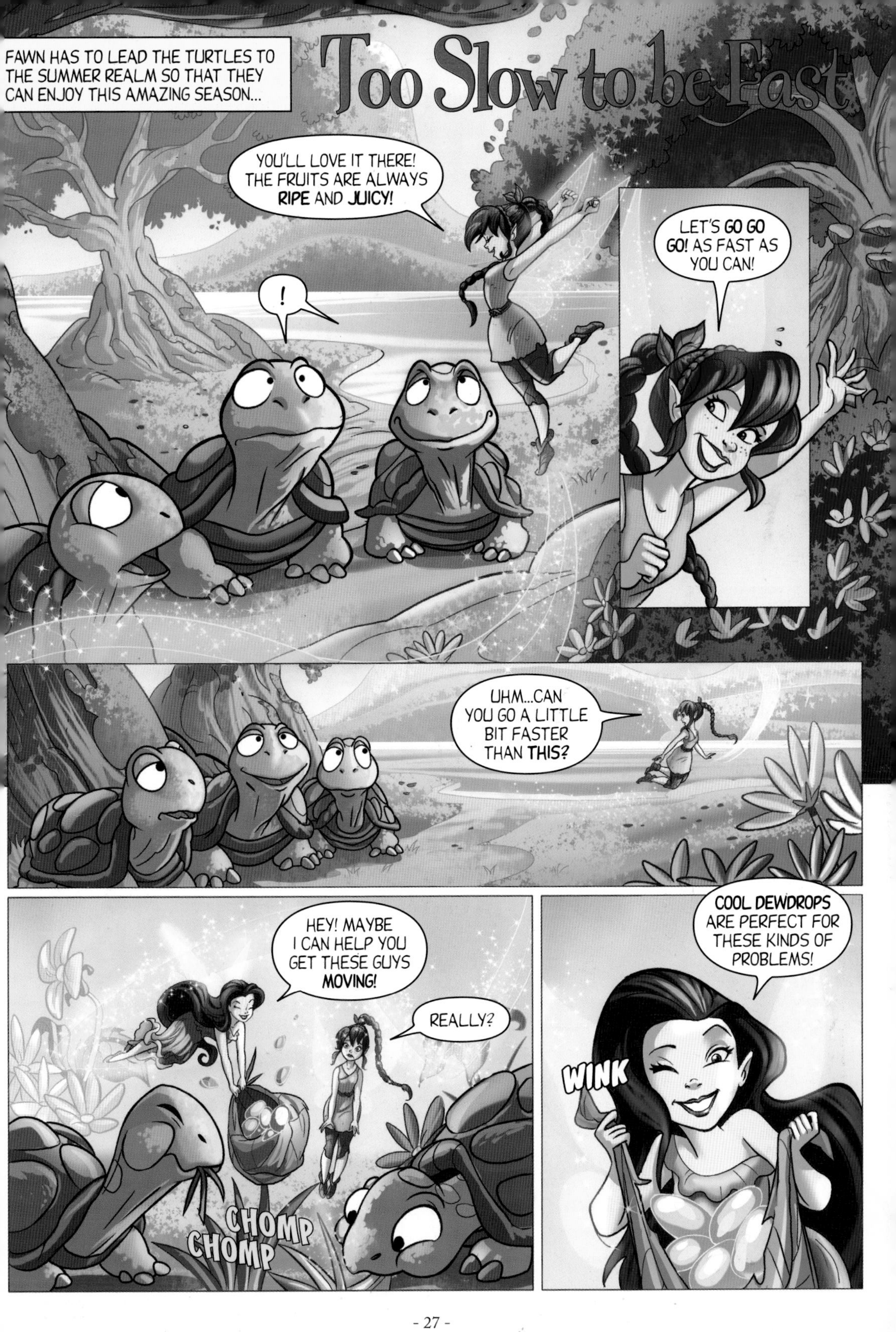

FAWN HAS TO LEAD THE TURTLES TO THE SUMMER REALM SO THAT THEY CAN ENJOY THIS AMAZING SEASON...
Too Slow to be Fast
YOU'LL LOVE IT THERE! THE FRUITS ARE ALWAYS RIPE AND JUICY!
!
LET'S GO GO GO! AS FAST AS YOU CAN!
UHM...CAN YOU GO A LITTLE BIT FASTER THAN THIS?
HEY! MAYBE I CAN HELP YOU GET THESE GUYS MOVING!
REALLY?
CHOMP
CHOMP
COOL DEWDROPS ARE PERFECT FOR THESE KINDS OF PROBLEMS!
WINK

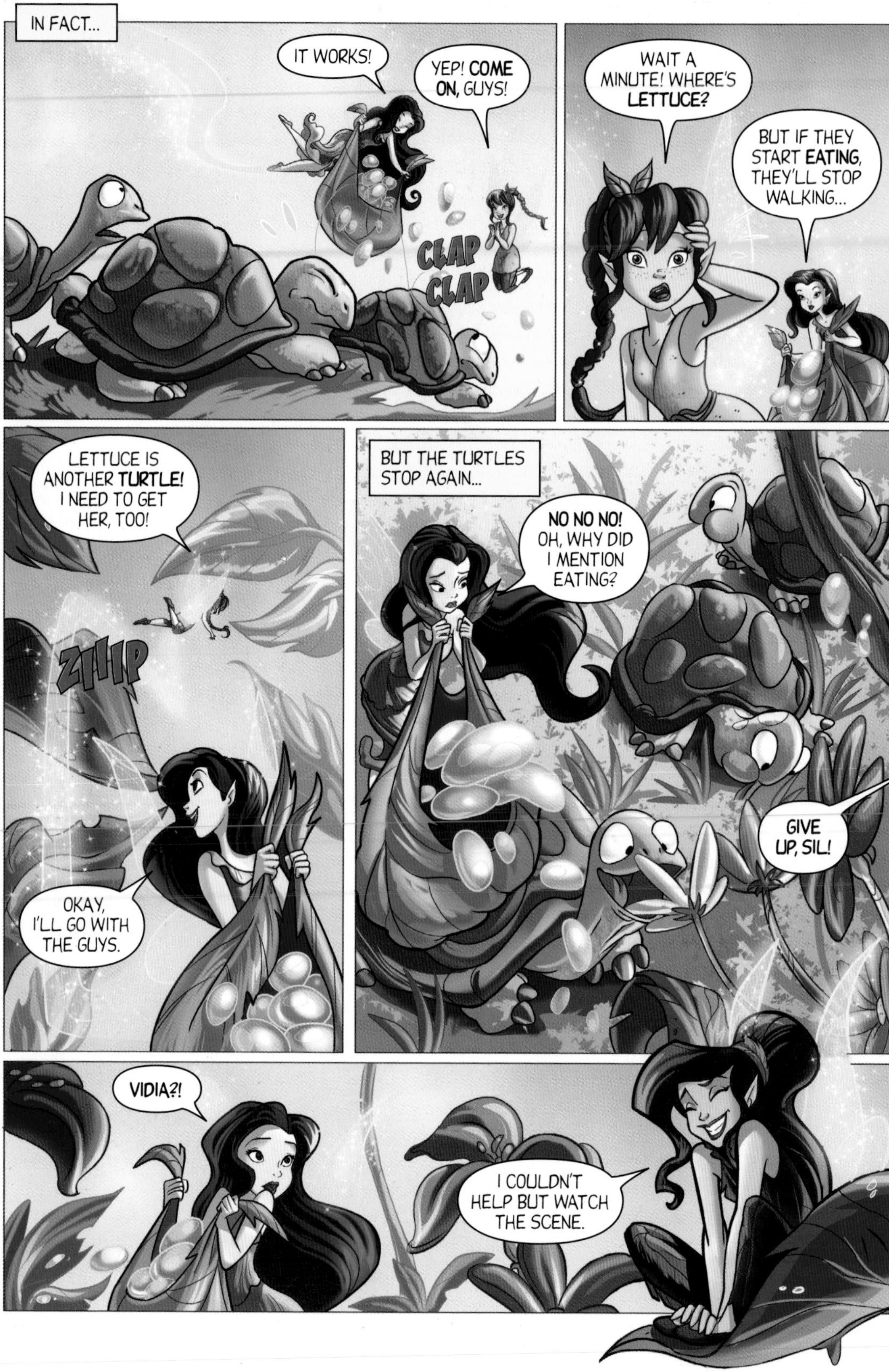
IN FACT...
IT WORKS!
YEP! COME ON, GUYS!
CLAP CLAP
WAIT A MINUTE! WHERE'S LETTUCE?
BUT IF THEY START EATING, THEY'LL STOP WALKING...
LETTUCE IS ANOTHER TURTLE! I NEED TO GET HER, TOO!
ZHIP
OKAY, I'LL GO WITH THE GUYS.
BUT THE TURTLES STOP AGAIN...
NO NO NO! OH, WHY DID I MENTION EATING?
GIVE UP, SIL!
VIDIA?!
I COULDN'T HELP BUT WATCH THE SCENE.

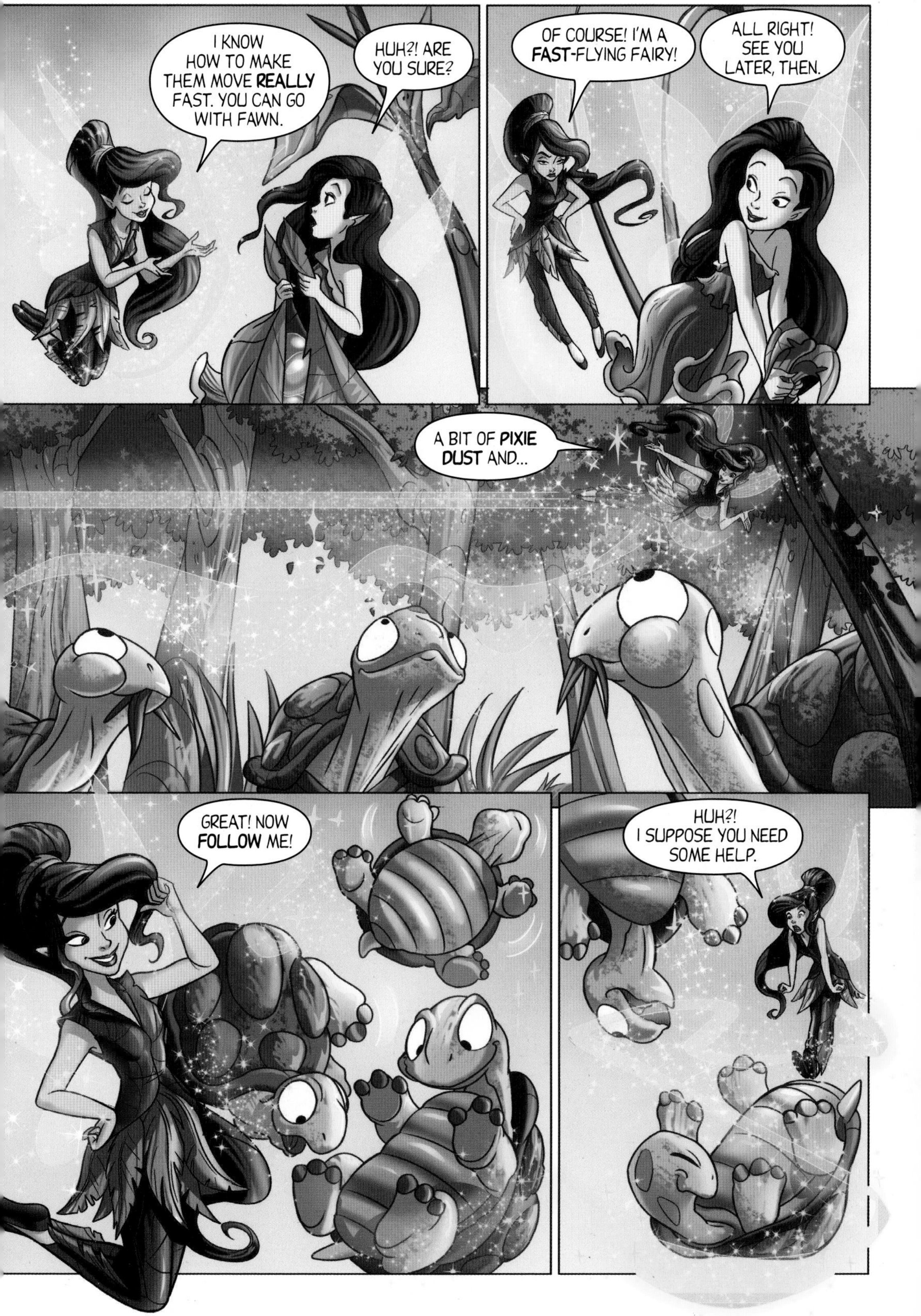
I KNOW HOW TO MAKE THEM MOVE REALLY FAST. YOU CAN GO WITH FAWN.
HUH?! ARE YOU SURE?
OF COURSE! I'M A FAST-FLYING FAIRY!
ALL RIGHT! SEE YOU LATER, THEN.
A BIT OF PIXIE DUST AND...
GREAT! NOW FOLLOW ME!
HUH?! I SUPPOSE YOU NEED SOME HELP.

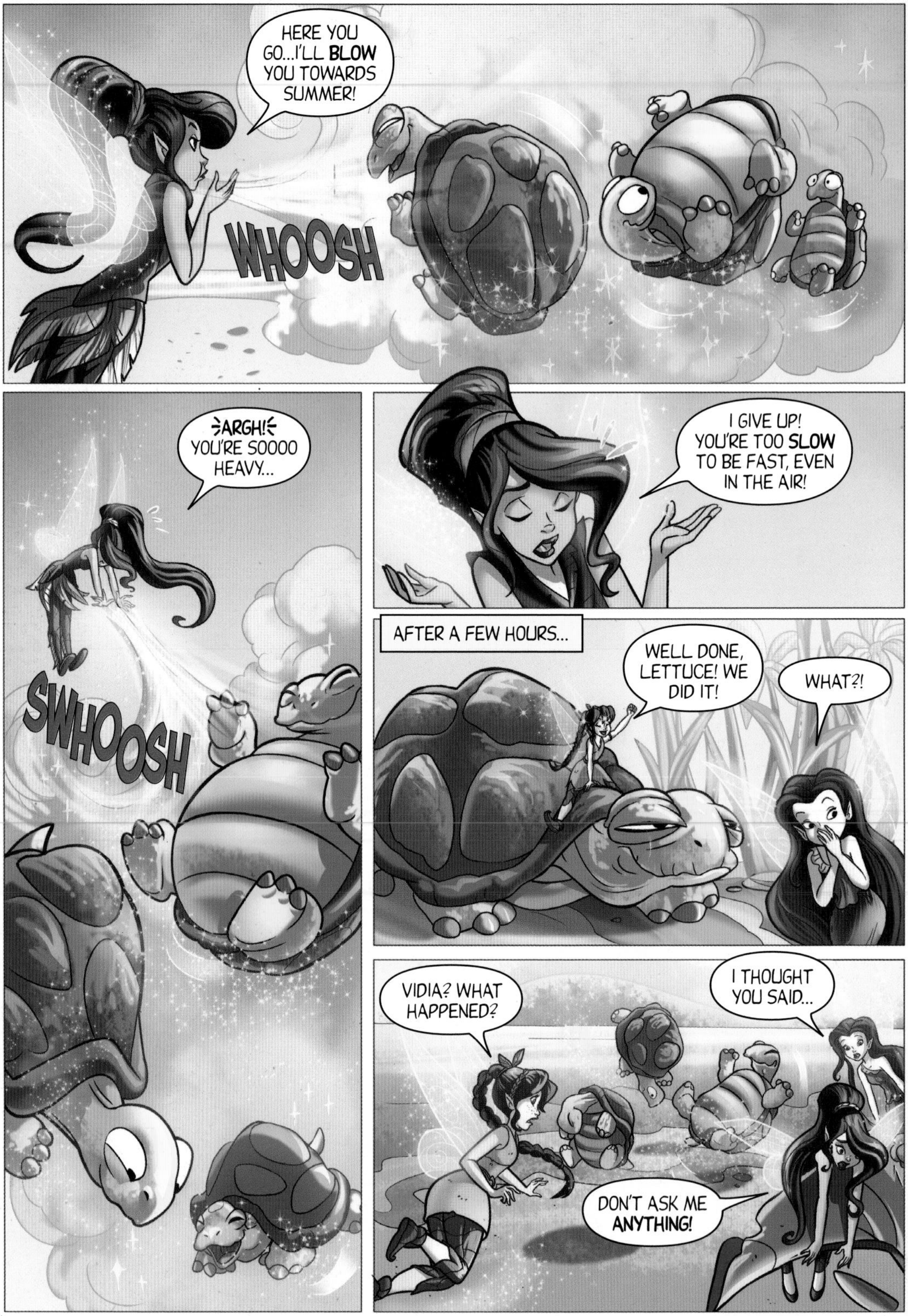
HERE YOU GO...I'LL BLOW YOU TOWARDS SUMMER!
WHOOSH
ARGH! YOU'RE SOOOO HEAVY...
SWHOOSH
I GIVE UP! YOU'RE TOO SLOW TO BE FAST, EVEN IN THE AIR!
AFTER A FEW HOURS...
WELL DONE, LETTUCE! WE DID IT!
WHAT?!
VIDIA? WHAT HAPPENED?
I THOUGHT YOU SAID...
DON'T ASK ME ANYTHING!

THE END

"Easy Gardening"

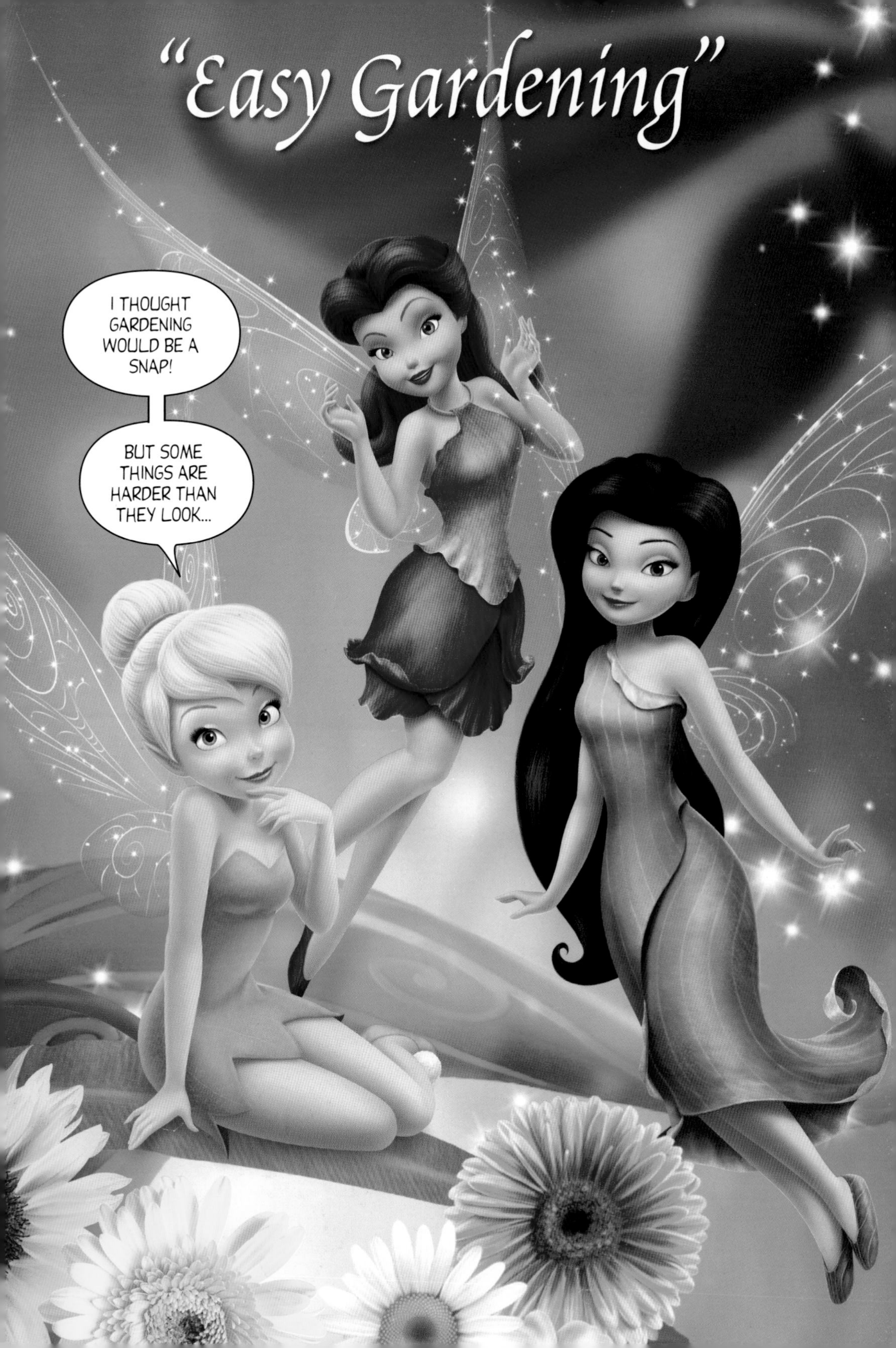
I THOUGHT GARDENING WOULD BE A SNAP!
BUT SOME THINGS ARE HARDER THAN THEY LOOK...

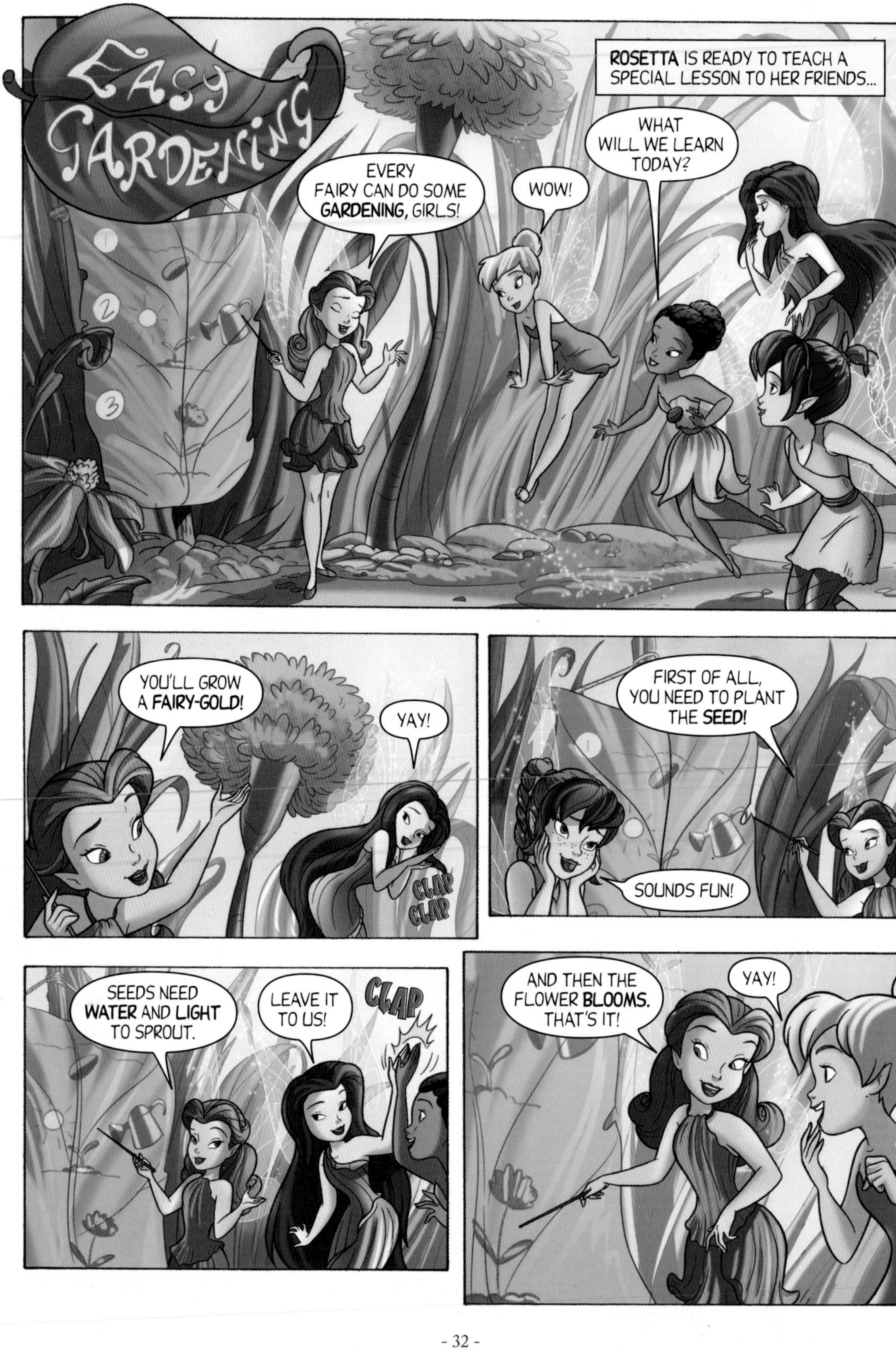
EASY GARDENING
ROSETTA IS READY TO TEACH A SPECIAL LESSON TO HER FRIENDS...
EVERY FAIRY CAN DO SOME GARDENING, GIRLS!
WOW!
WHAT WILL WE LEARN TODAY?
YOU'LL GROW A FAIRY-GOLD!
YAY!
CLAP CLAP
FIRST OF ALL, YOU NEED TO PLANT THE SEED!
SOUNDS FUN!
SEEDS NEED WATER AND LIGHT TO SPROUT.
LEAVE IT TO US!
CLAP
AND THEN THE FLOWER BLOOMS. THAT'S IT!
YAY!

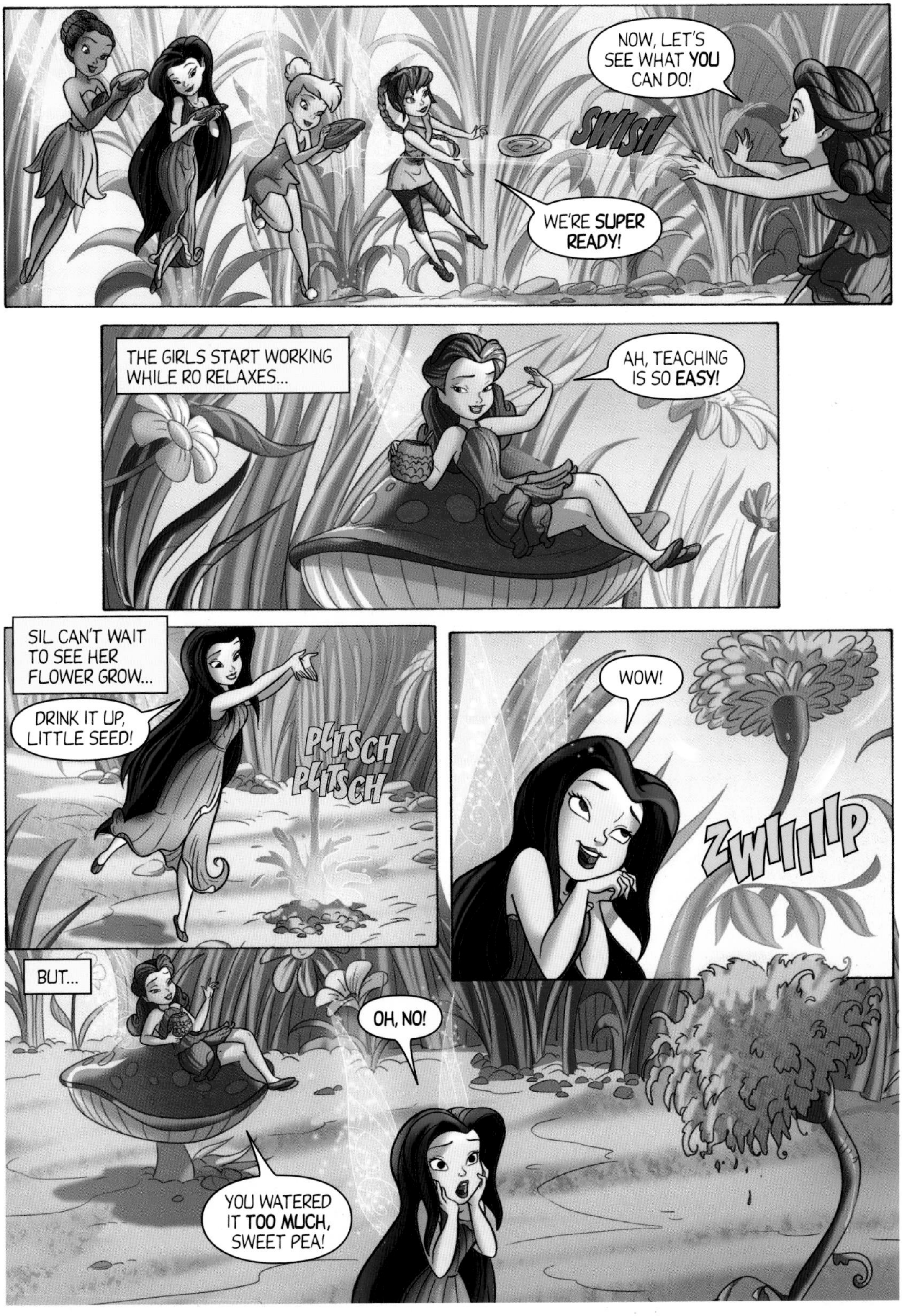
NOW, LET'S SEE WHAT YOU CAN DO!
SWISH
WE'RE SUPER READY!
THE GIRLS START WORKING WHILE RO RELAXES...
AH, TEACHING IS SO EASY!
SIL CAN'T WAIT TO SEE HER FLOWER GROW...
DRINK IT UP, LITTLE SEED!
PLITSCH
PLITSCH
WOW!
ZWIIIIIP
BUT...
OH, NO!
YOU WATERED IT TOO MUCH, SWEET PEA!

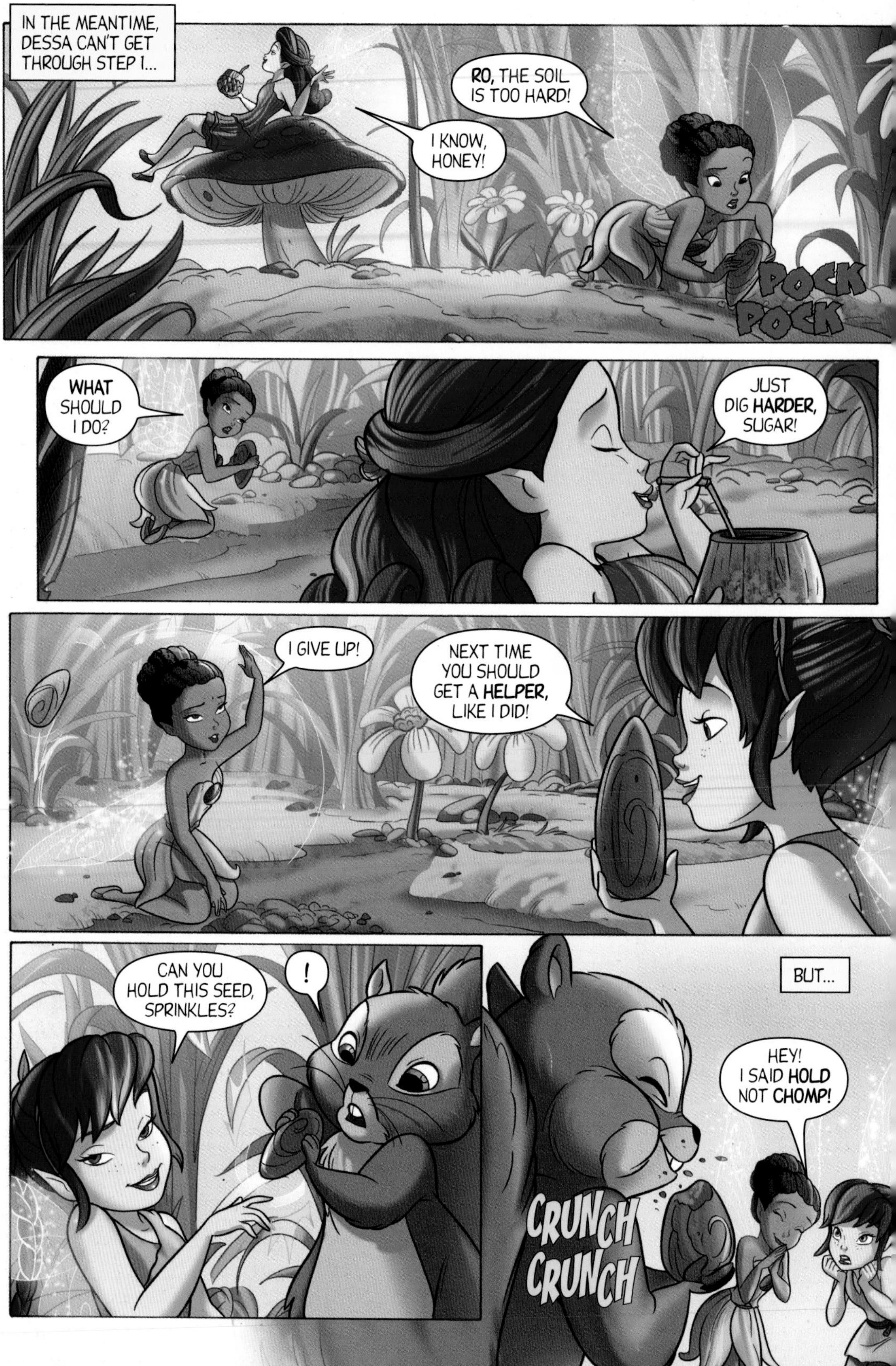

IN THE MEANTIME, DESSA CAN'T GET THROUGH STEP 1...
RO, THE SOIL IS TOO HARD!
I KNOW, HONEY!
POCK POCK
WHAT SHOULD I DO?
JUST DIG HARDER, SUGAR!
I GIVE UP!
NEXT TIME YOU SHOULD GET A HELPER, LIKE I DID!
CAN YOU HOLD THIS SEED, SPRINKLES?
!
BUT...
HEY! I SAID HOLD NOT CHOMP!
CRUNCH CRUNCH

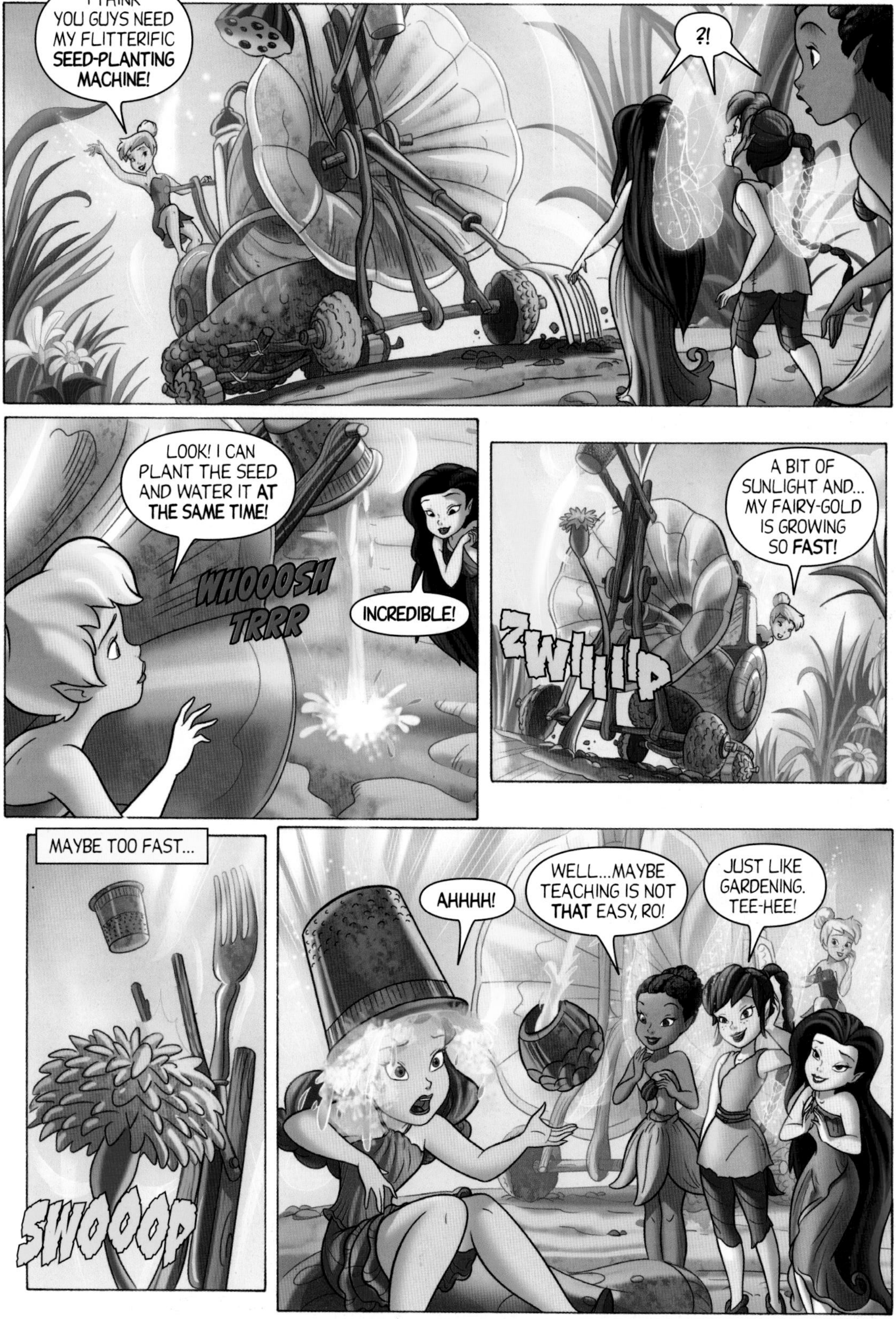
I THINK YOU GUYS NEED MY FLITTERIFIC **SEED-PLANTING MACHINE!**
?!
LOOK! I CAN PLANT THE SEED AND WATER IT **AT THE SAME TIME!**
WHOOOSH
TRRR
INCREDIBLE!
A BIT OF SUNLIGHT AND... MY FAIRY-GOLD IS GROWING SO **FAST!**
ZWIIIIP
MAYBE TOO FAST...
SWOOOP
AHHHH!
WELL...MAYBE TEACHING IS NOT **THAT** EASY, RO!
JUST LIKE GARDENING. TEE-HEE!

THE END

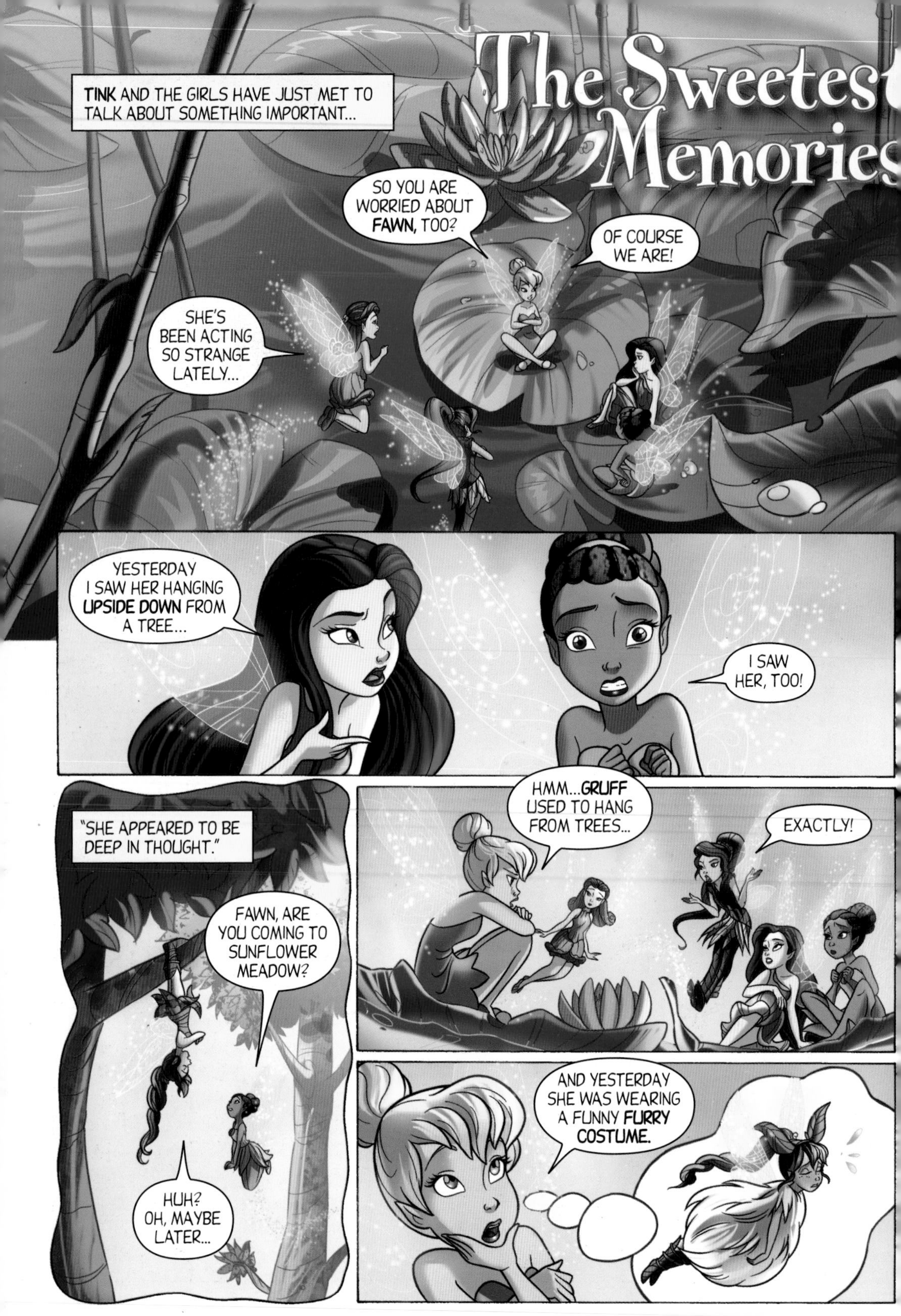
The Sweetest Memories
TINK AND THE GIRLS HAVE JUST MET TO TALK ABOUT SOMETHING IMPORTANT...
SO YOU ARE WORRIED ABOUT FAWN, TOO?
OF COURSE WE ARE!
SHE'S BEEN ACTING SO STRANGE LATELY...
YESTERDAY I SAW HER HANGING UPSIDE DOWN FROM A TREE...
I SAW HER, TOO!
"SHE APPEARED TO BE DEEP IN THOUGHT."
FAWN, ARE YOU COMING TO SUNFLOWER MEADOW?
HUH? OH, MAYBE LATER...
HMM...GRUFF USED TO HANG FROM TREES...
EXACTLY!
AND YESTERDAY SHE WAS WEARING A FUNNY FURRY COSTUME.

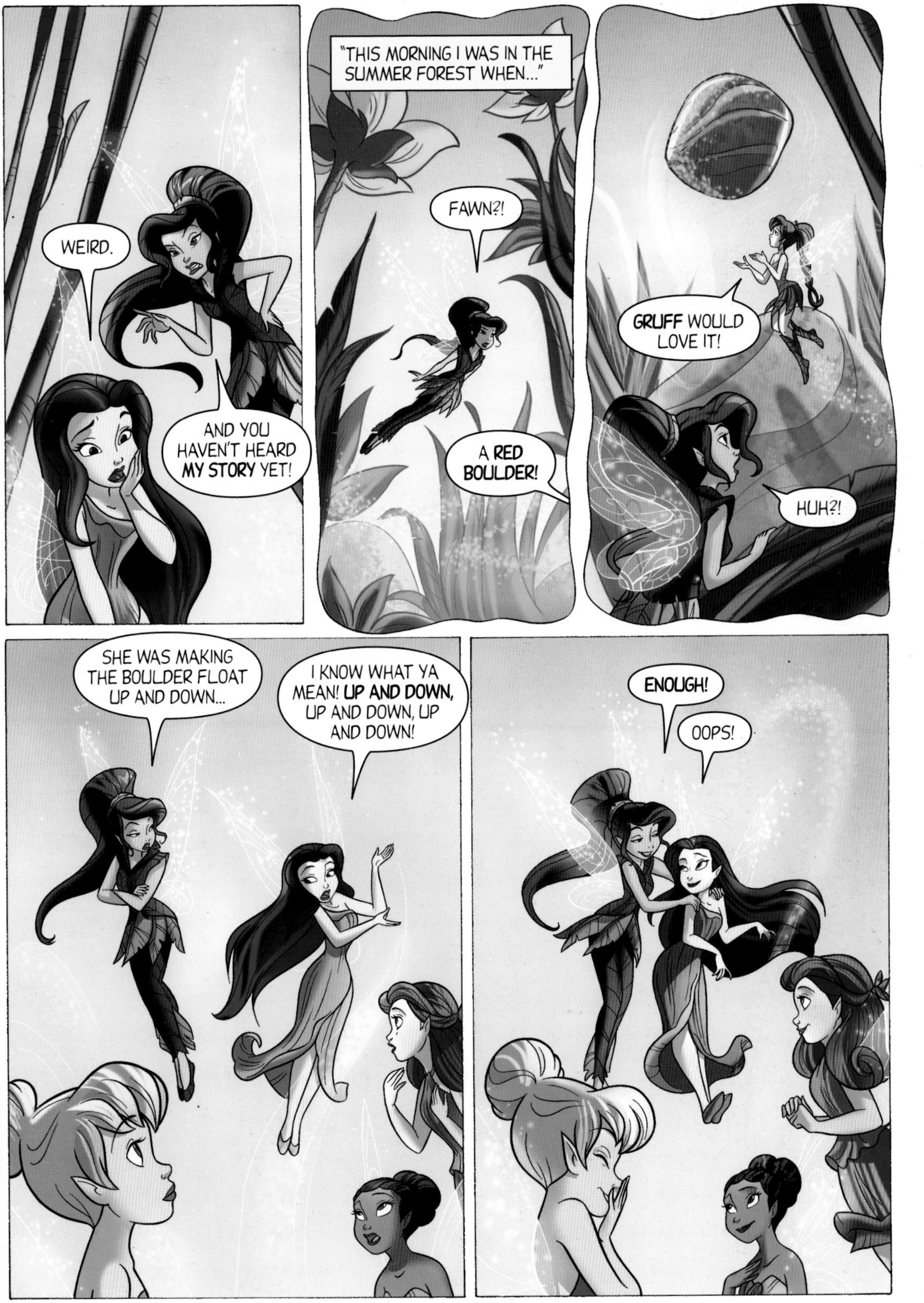
WEIRD.
AND YOU HAVEN'T HEARD MY STORY YET!
"THIS MORNING I WAS IN THE SUMMER FOREST WHEN..."
FAWN?!
A RED BOULDER!
GRUFF WOULD LOVE IT!
HUH?!
SHE WAS MAKING THE BOULDER FLOAT UP AND DOWN...
I KNOW WHAT YA MEAN! UP AND DOWN, UP AND DOWN, UP AND DOWN!
ENOUGH!
OOPS!

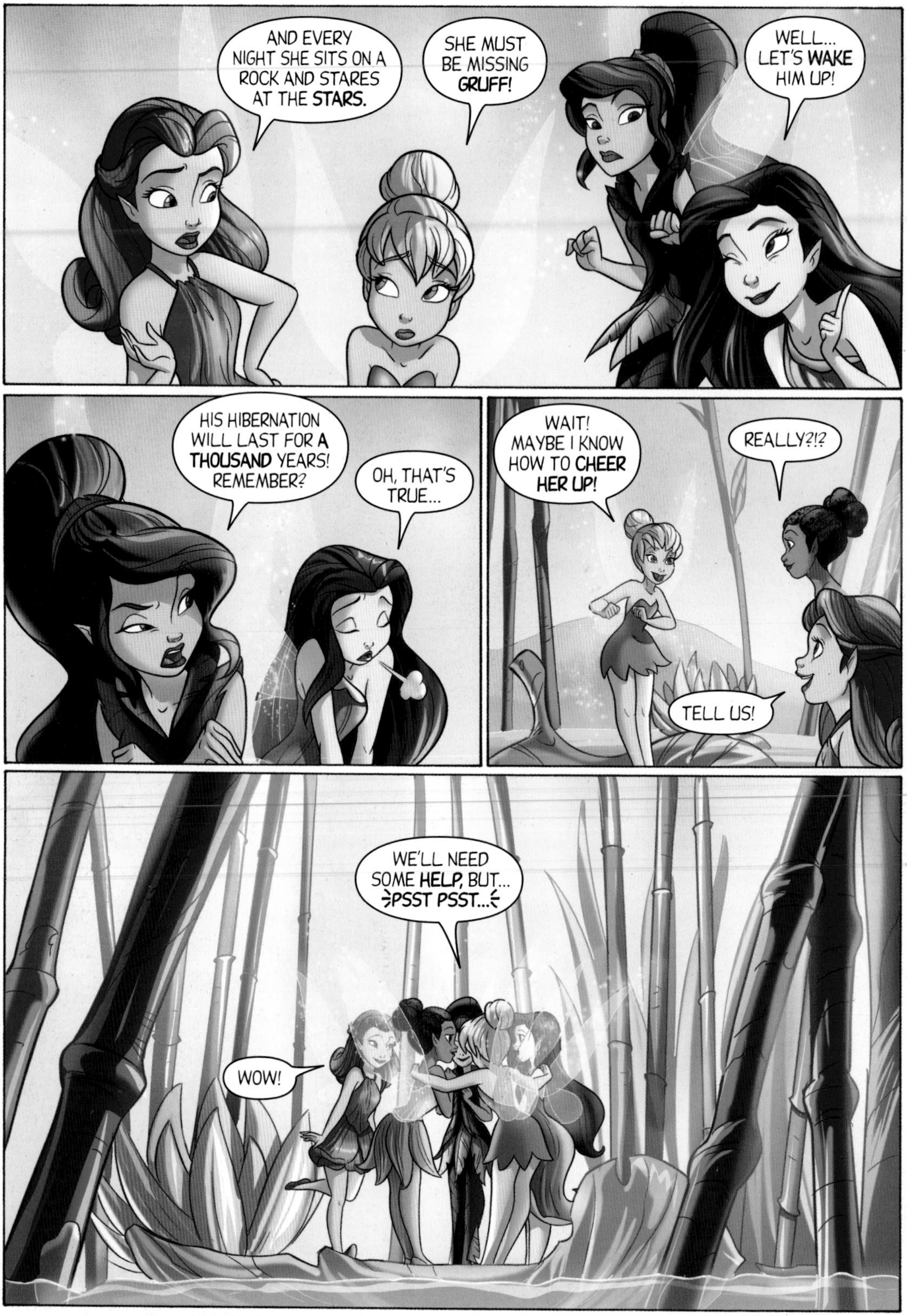
AND EVERY NIGHT SHE SITS ON A ROCK AND STARES AT THE STARS.
SHE MUST BE MISSING GRUFF!
WELL... LET'S WAKE HIM UP!
HIS HIBERNATION WILL LAST FOR A THOUSAND YEARS! REMEMBER?
OH, THAT'S TRUE...
WAIT! MAYBE I KNOW HOW TO CHEER HER UP!
REALLY?!?
TELL US!
WE'LL NEED SOME HELP, BUT... PSST PSST...
WOW!

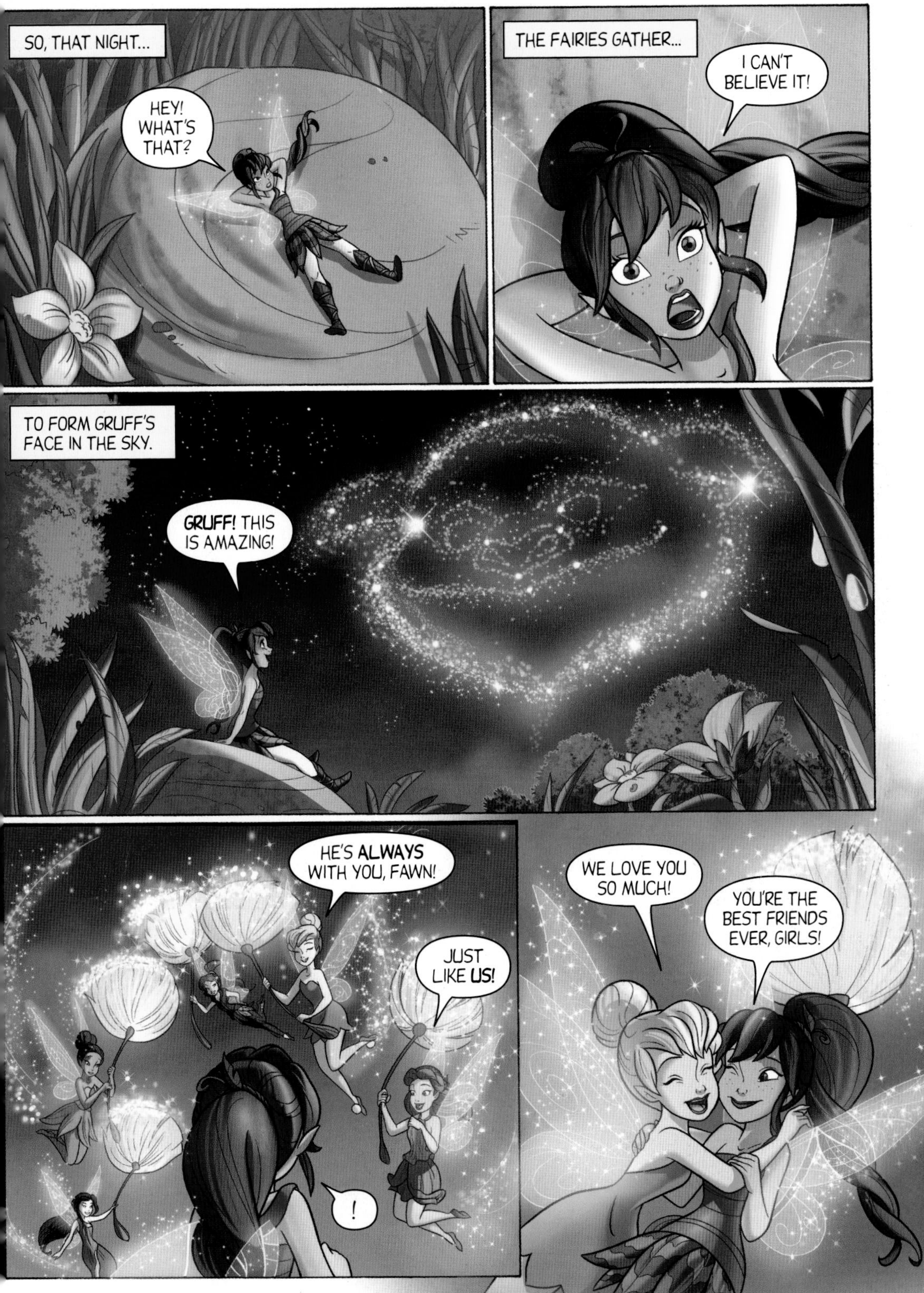

SO, THAT NIGHT...
HEY! WHAT'S THAT?
THE FAIRIES GATHER...
I CAN'T BELIEVE IT!
TO FORM GRUFF'S FACE IN THE SKY.
GRUFF! THIS IS AMAZING!
HE'S **ALWAYS** WITH YOU, FAWN!
JUST LIKE **US!**
!
WE LOVE YOU SO MUCH!
YOU'RE THE BEST FRIENDS EVER, GIRLS!
THE END

What Counts the Most

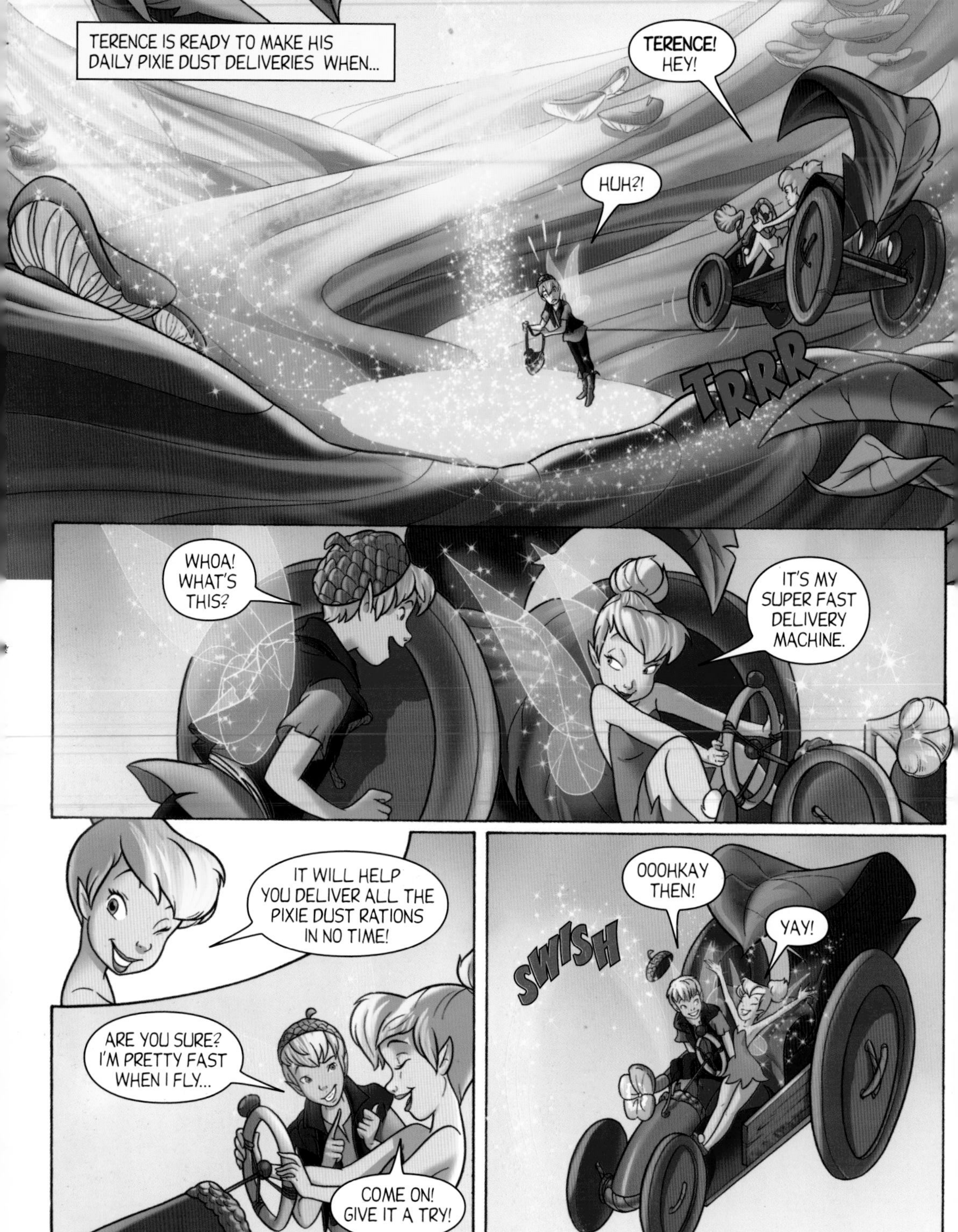

TERENCE IS READY TO MAKE HIS DAILY PIXIE DUST DELIVERIES WHEN...
TERENCE! HEY!
HUH?!
TRRR
WHOA! WHAT'S THIS?
IT'S MY SUPER FAST DELIVERY MACHINE.
IT WILL HELP YOU DELIVER ALL THE PIXIE DUST RATIONS IN NO TIME!
ARE YOU SURE? I'M PRETTY FAST WHEN I FLY...
COME ON! GIVE IT A TRY!
OOOHKAY THEN!
YAY!
SWISH

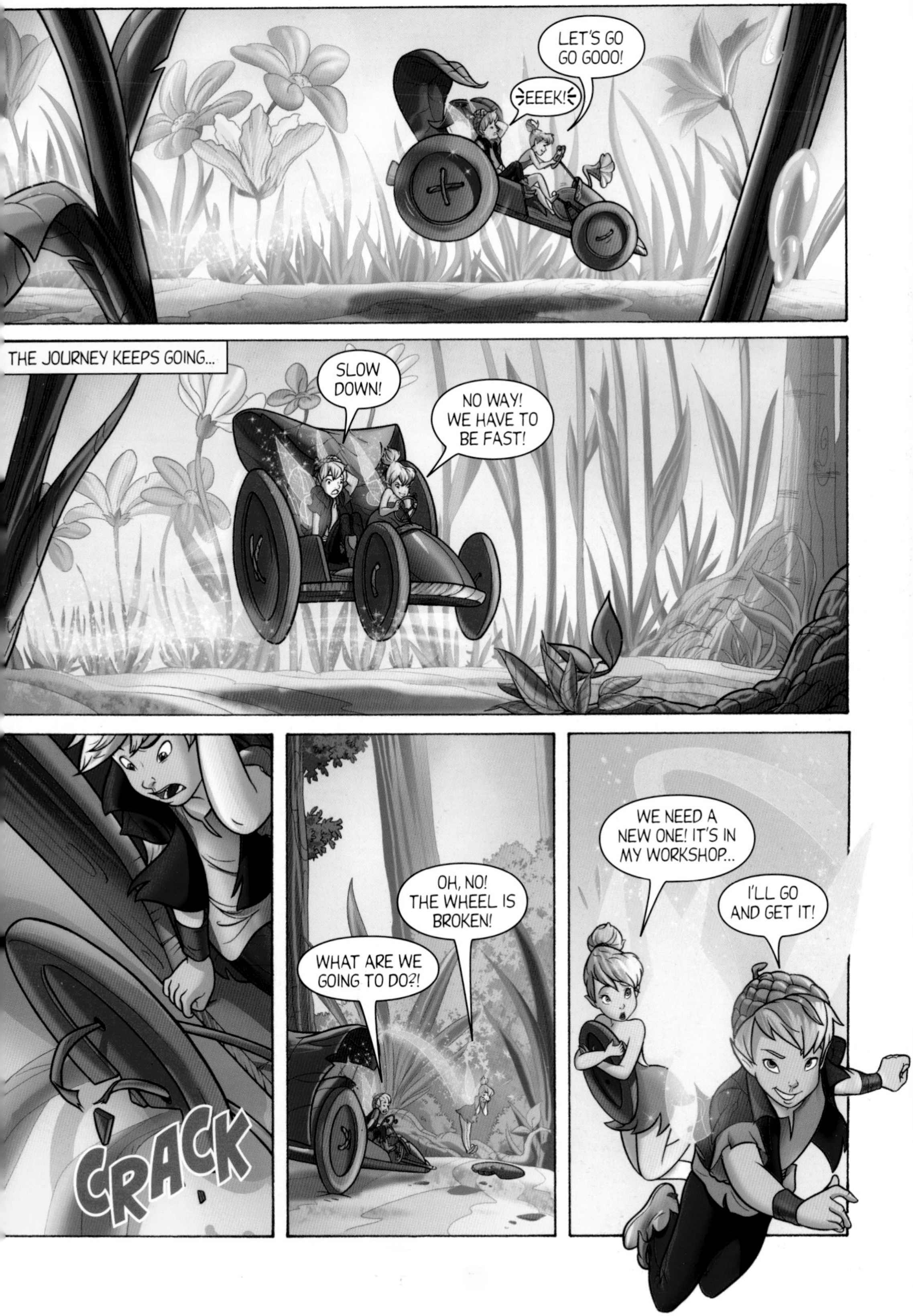

EEEK!
LET'S GO GO GOOO!
THE JOURNEY KEEPS GOING...
SLOW DOWN!
NO WAY! WE HAVE TO BE FAST!
CRACK
OH, NO! THE WHEEL IS BROKEN!
WHAT ARE WE GOING TO DO?!
WE NEED A NEW ONE! IT'S IN MY WORKSHOP...
I'LL GO AND GET IT!

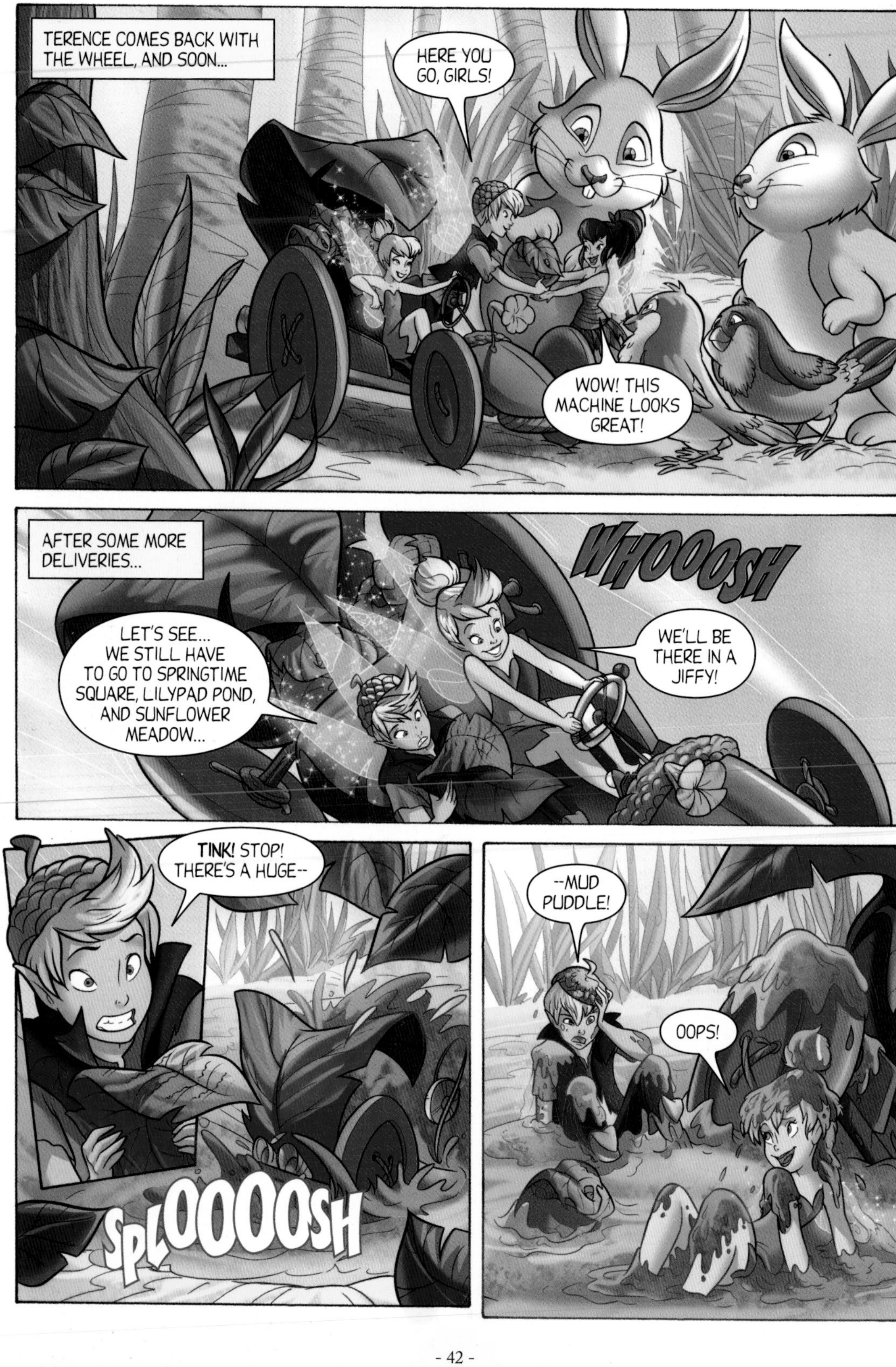

TERENCE COMES BACK WITH THE WHEEL, AND SOON...
HERE YOU GO, GIRLS!
WOW! THIS MACHINE LOOKS GREAT!
AFTER SOME MORE DELIVERIES...
WHOOOOSH
LET'S SEE... WE STILL HAVE TO GO TO SPRINGTIME SQUARE, LILYPAD POND, AND SUNFLOWER MEADOW...
WE'LL BE THERE IN A JIFFY!
TINK! STOP! THERE'S A HUGE--
SPLOOOOSH
--MUD PUDDLE!
OOPS!

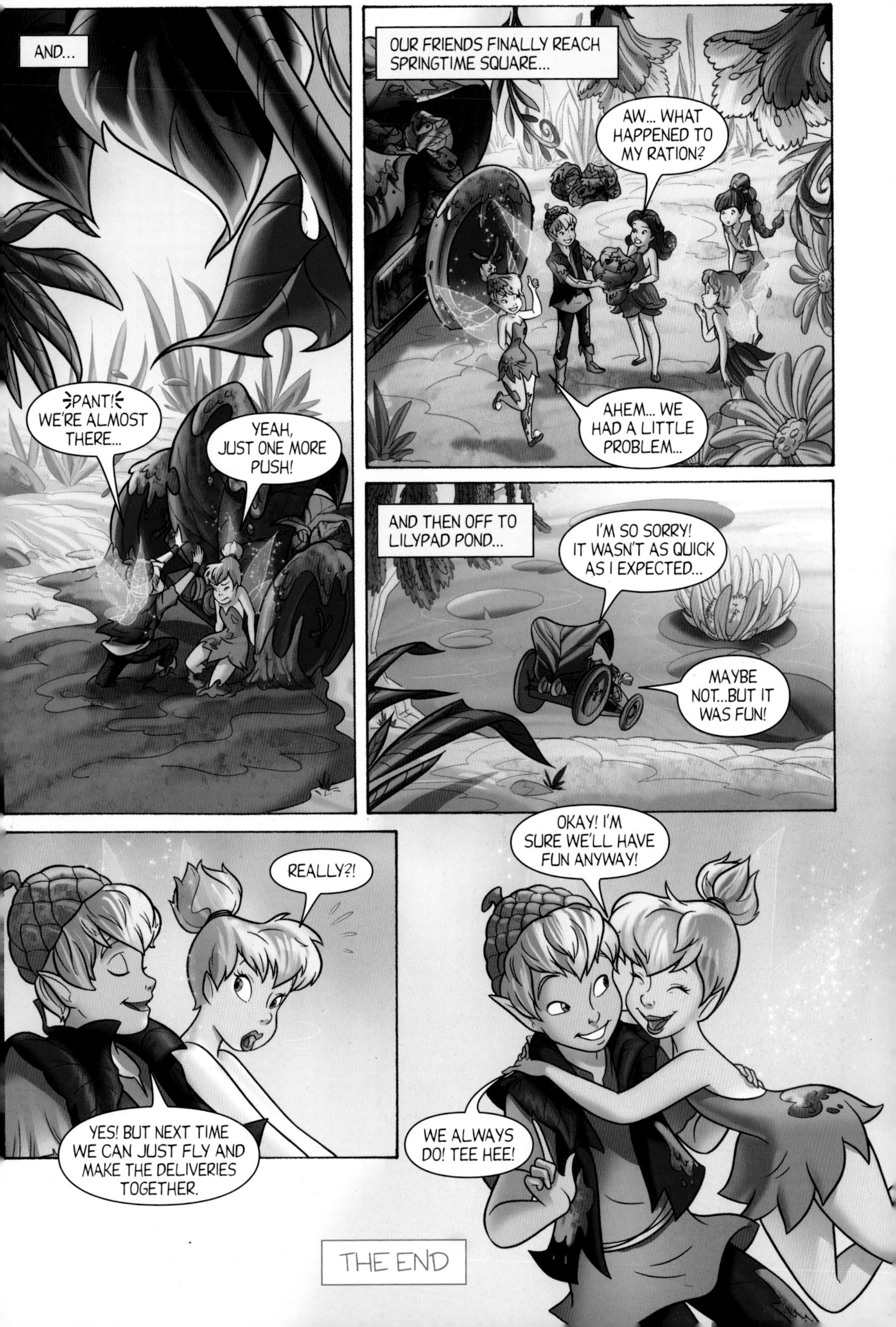
AND...
OUR FRIENDS FINALLY REACH SPRINGTIME SQUARE...
AW... WHAT HAPPENED TO MY RATION?
AHEM... WE HAD A LITTLE PROBLEM...
PANT! WE'RE ALMOST THERE...
YEAH, JUST ONE MORE PUSH!
AND THEN OFF TO LILYPAD POND...
I'M SO SORRY! IT WASN'T AS QUICK AS I EXPECTED...
MAYBE NOT...BUT IT WAS FUN!
REALLY?!
YES! BUT NEXT TIME WE CAN JUST FLY AND MAKE THE DELIVERIES TOGETHER.
OKAY! I'M SURE WE'LL HAVE FUN ANYWAY!
WE ALWAYS DO! TEE HEE!
THE END

"A Sudden Allergy"

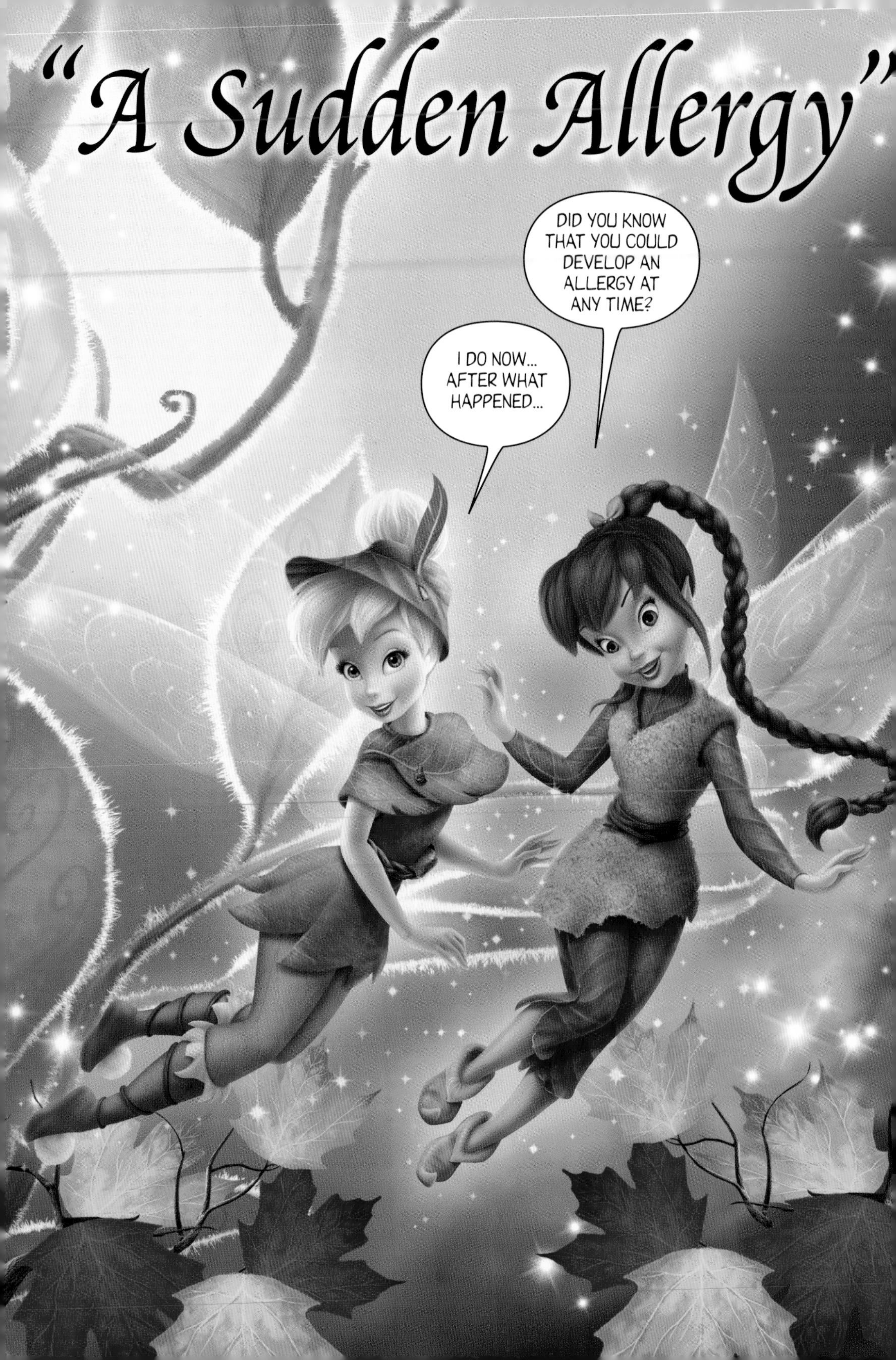
DID YOU KNOW THAT YOU COULD DEVELOP AN ALLERGY AT ANY TIME?
I DO NOW... AFTER WHAT HAPPENED...

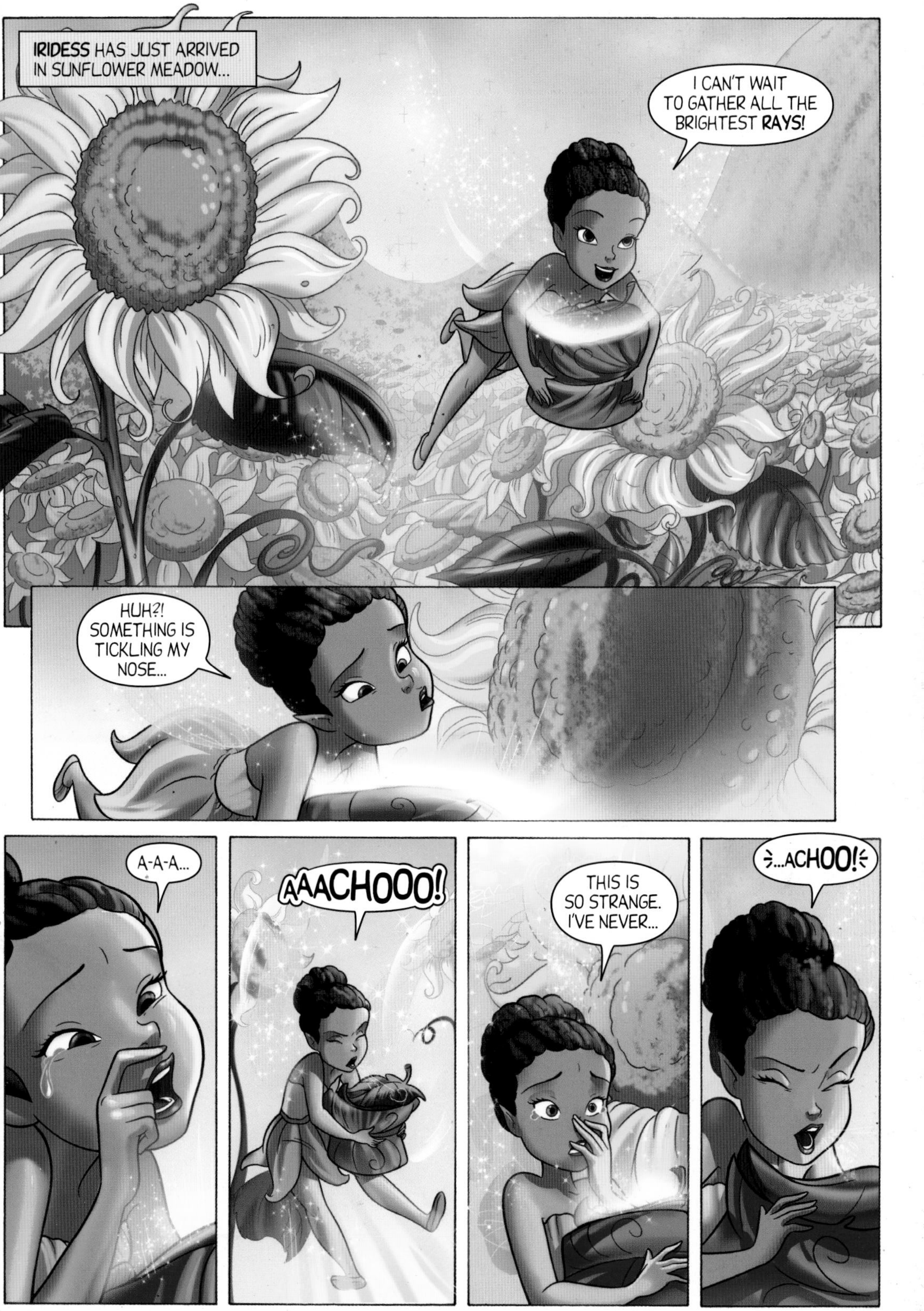
IRIDESS HAS JUST ARRIVED IN SUNFLOWER MEADOW...
I CAN'T WAIT TO GATHER ALL THE BRIGHTEST RAYS!
HUH?! SOMETHING IS TICKLING MY NOSE...
A-A-A...
AAACHOOO!
THIS IS SO STRANGE. I'VE NEVER...
...ACHOO!

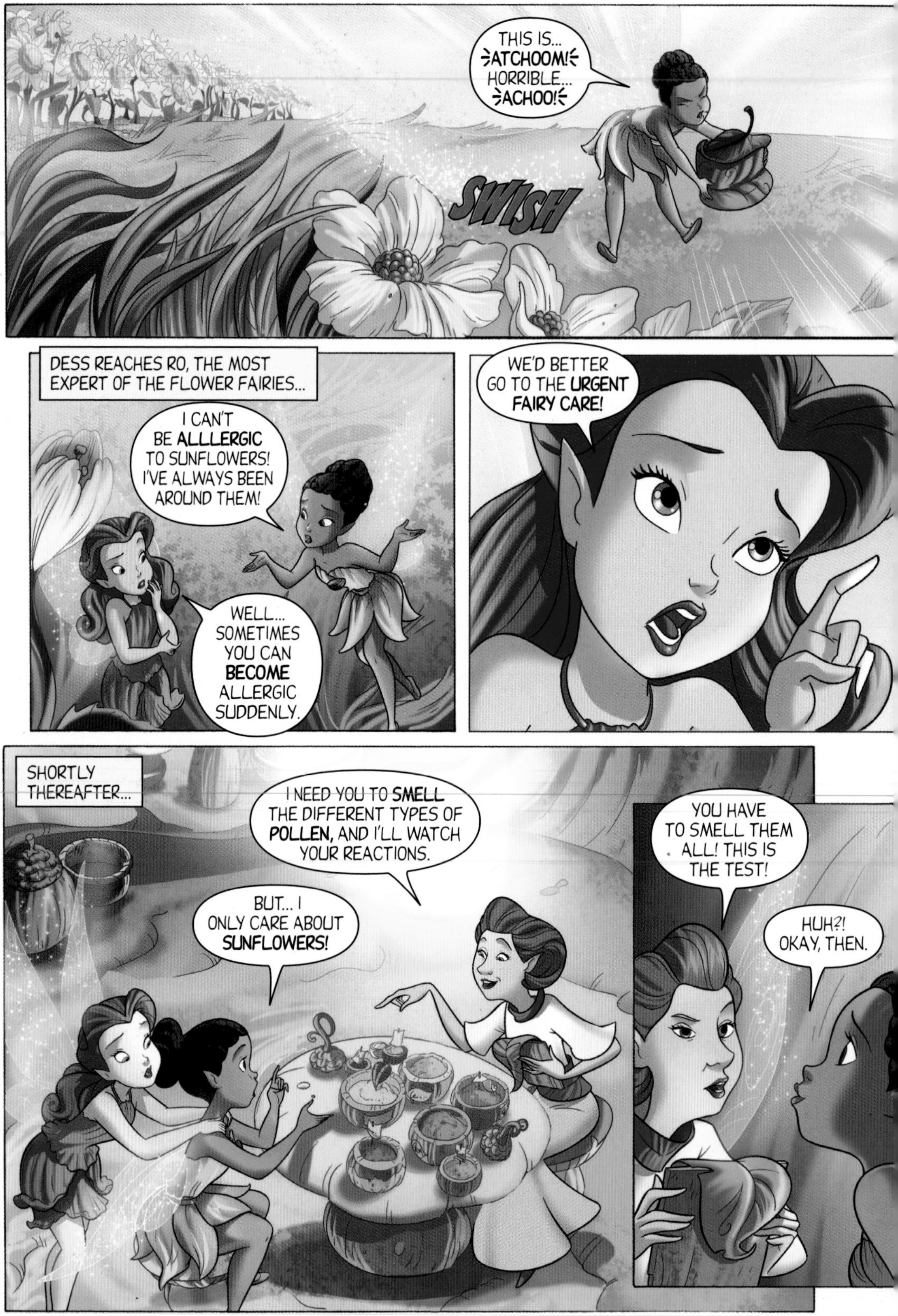
THIS IS... ATCHOOM! HORRIBLE... ACHOO!
SWISH
DESS REACHES RO, THE MOST EXPERT OF THE FLOWER FAIRIES...
I CAN'T BE ALLLERGIC TO SUNFLOWERS! I'VE ALWAYS BEEN AROUND THEM!
WELL... SOMETIMES YOU CAN BECOME ALLERGIC SUDDENLY.
WE'D BETTER GO TO THE URGENT FAIRY CARE!
SHORTLY THEREAFTER...
I NEED YOU TO SMELL THE DIFFERENT TYPES OF POLLEN, AND I'LL WATCH YOUR REACTIONS.
BUT... I ONLY CARE ABOUT SUNFLOWERS!
YOU HAVE TO SMELL THEM ALL! THIS IS THE TEST!
HUH?! OKAY, THEN.

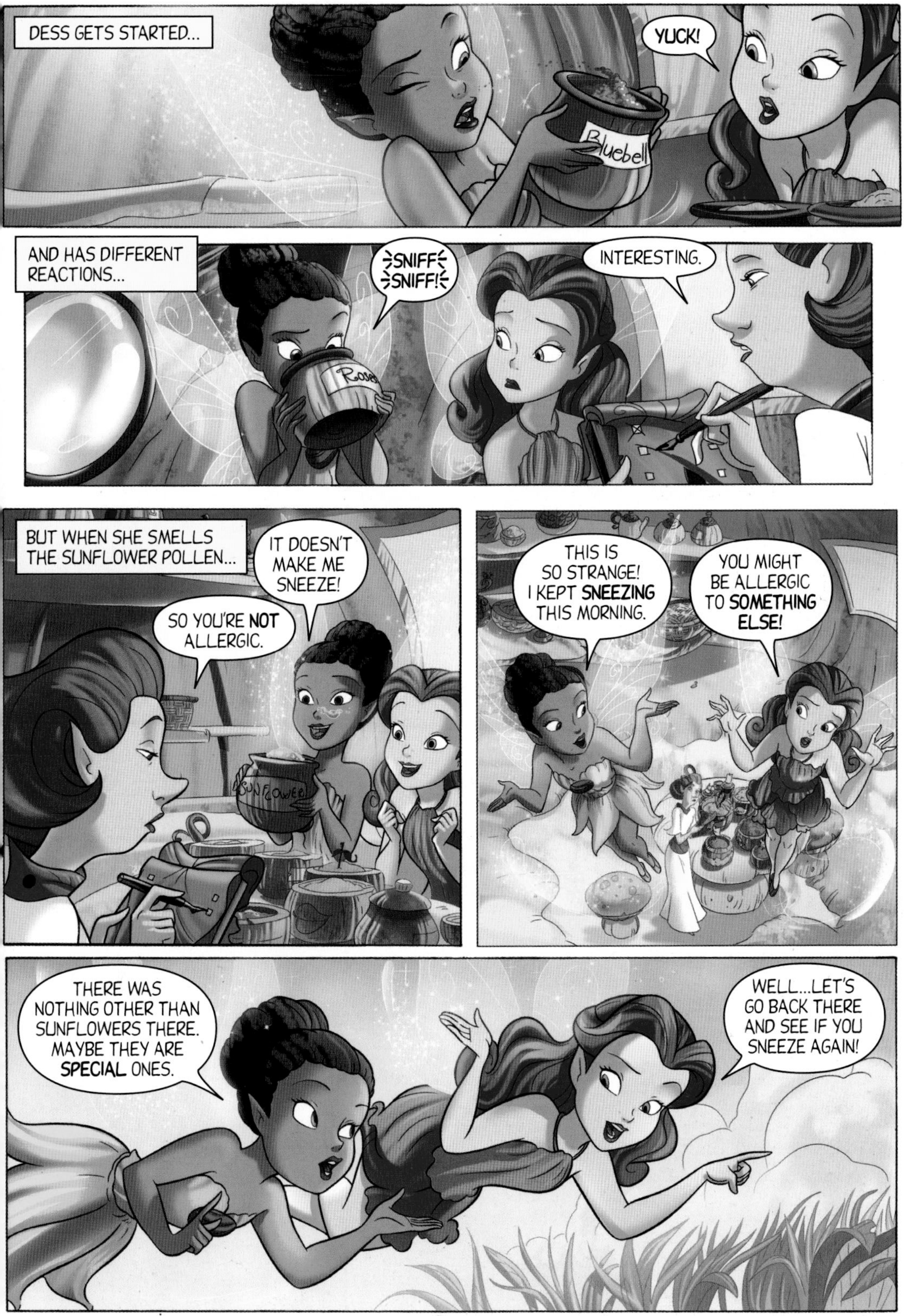
DESS GETS STARTED...
YUCK!
Bluebell
AND HAS DIFFERENT REACTIONS...
SNIFF SNIFF!
INTERESTING.
BUT WHEN SHE SMELLS THE SUNFLOWER POLLEN...
IT DOESN'T MAKE ME SNEEZE!
SO YOU'RE **NOT** ALLERGIC.
SUNFLOWER
THIS IS SO STRANGE! I KEPT **SNEEZING** THIS MORNING.
YOU MIGHT BE ALLERGIC TO **SOMETHING ELSE!**
THERE WAS NOTHING OTHER THAN SUNFLOWERS THERE. MAYBE THEY ARE **SPECIAL** ONES.
WELL...LET'S GO BACK THERE AND SEE IF YOU SNEEZE AGAIN!

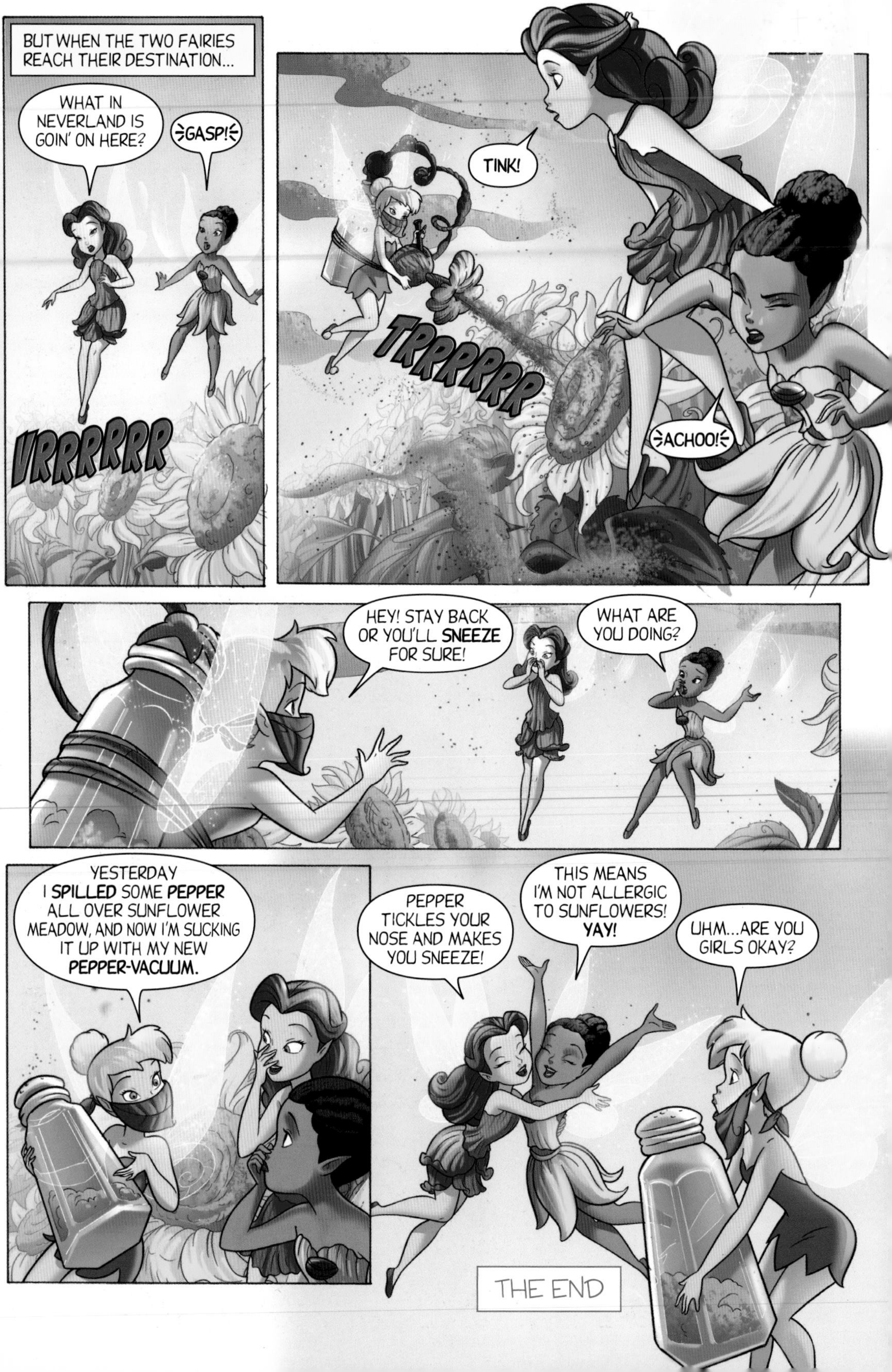
BUT WHEN THE TWO FAIRIES REACH THEIR DESTINATION...
WHAT IN NEVERLAND IS GOIN' ON HERE?
GASP!
VRRRRRR
TINK!
TRRRRRRR
ACHOO!
HEY! STAY BACK OR YOU'LL SNEEZE FOR SURE!
WHAT ARE YOU DOING?
YESTERDAY I SPILLED SOME PEPPER ALL OVER SUNFLOWER MEADOW, AND NOW I'M SUCKING IT UP WITH MY NEW PEPPER-VACUUM.
PEPPER TICKLES YOUR NOSE AND MAKES YOU SNEEZE!
THIS MEANS I'M NOT ALLERGIC TO SUNFLOWERS! YAY!
UHM...ARE YOU GIRLS OKAY?
THE END

The Surprise Party

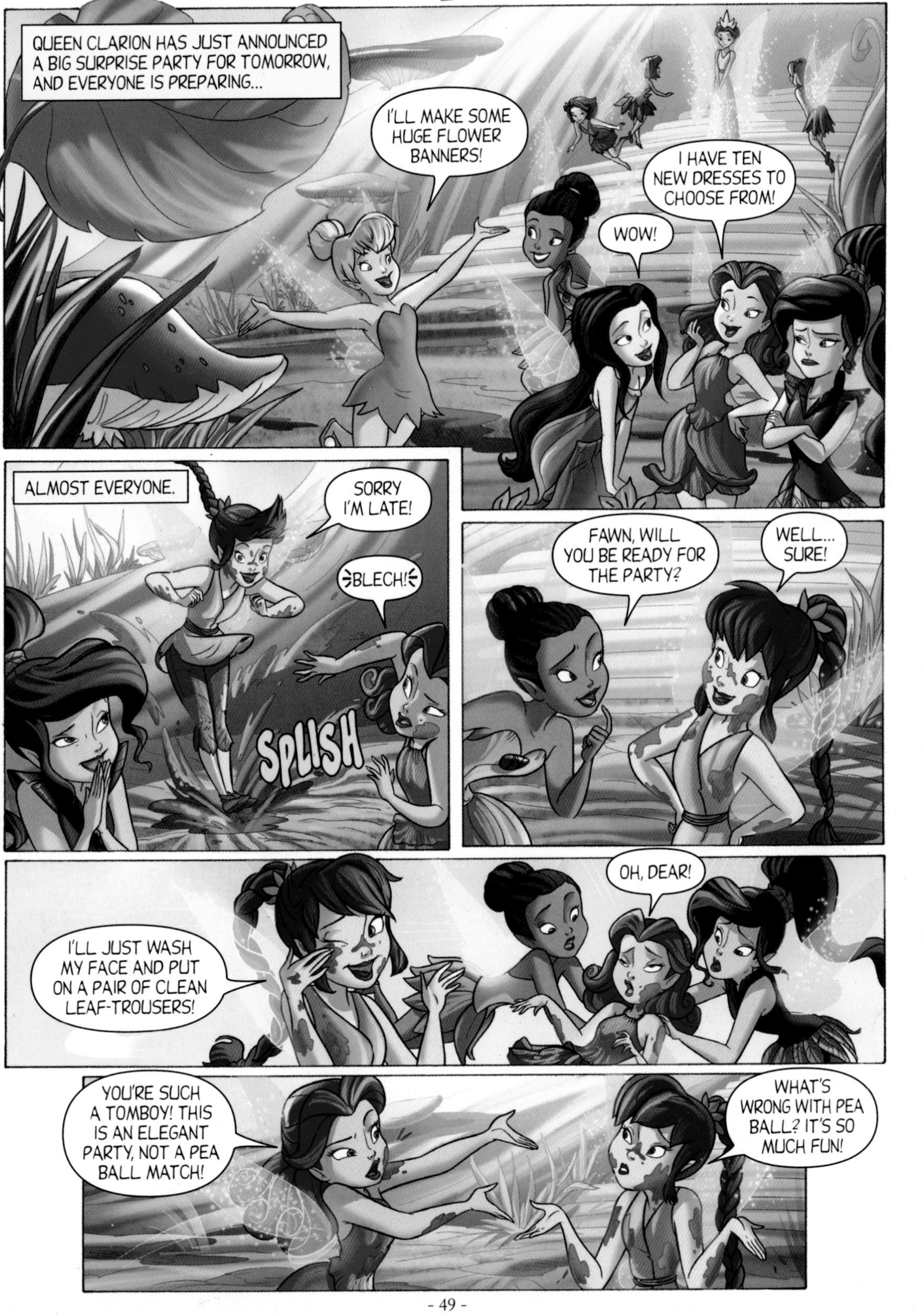
QUEEN CLARION HAS JUST ANNOUNCED A BIG SURPRISE PARTY FOR TOMORROW, AND EVERYONE IS PREPARING...
I'LL MAKE SOME HUGE FLOWER BANNERS!
I HAVE TEN NEW DRESSES TO CHOOSE FROM!
WOW!
ALMOST EVERYONE.
SORRY I'M LATE!
BLECH!
SPLISH
FAWN, WILL YOU BE READY FOR THE PARTY?
WELL... SURE!
OH, DEAR!
I'LL JUST WASH MY FACE AND PUT ON A PAIR OF CLEAN LEAF-TROUSERS!
YOU'RE SUCH A TOMBOY! THIS IS AN ELEGANT PARTY, NOT A PEA BALL MATCH!
WHAT'S WRONG WITH PEA BALL? IT'S SO MUCH FUN!

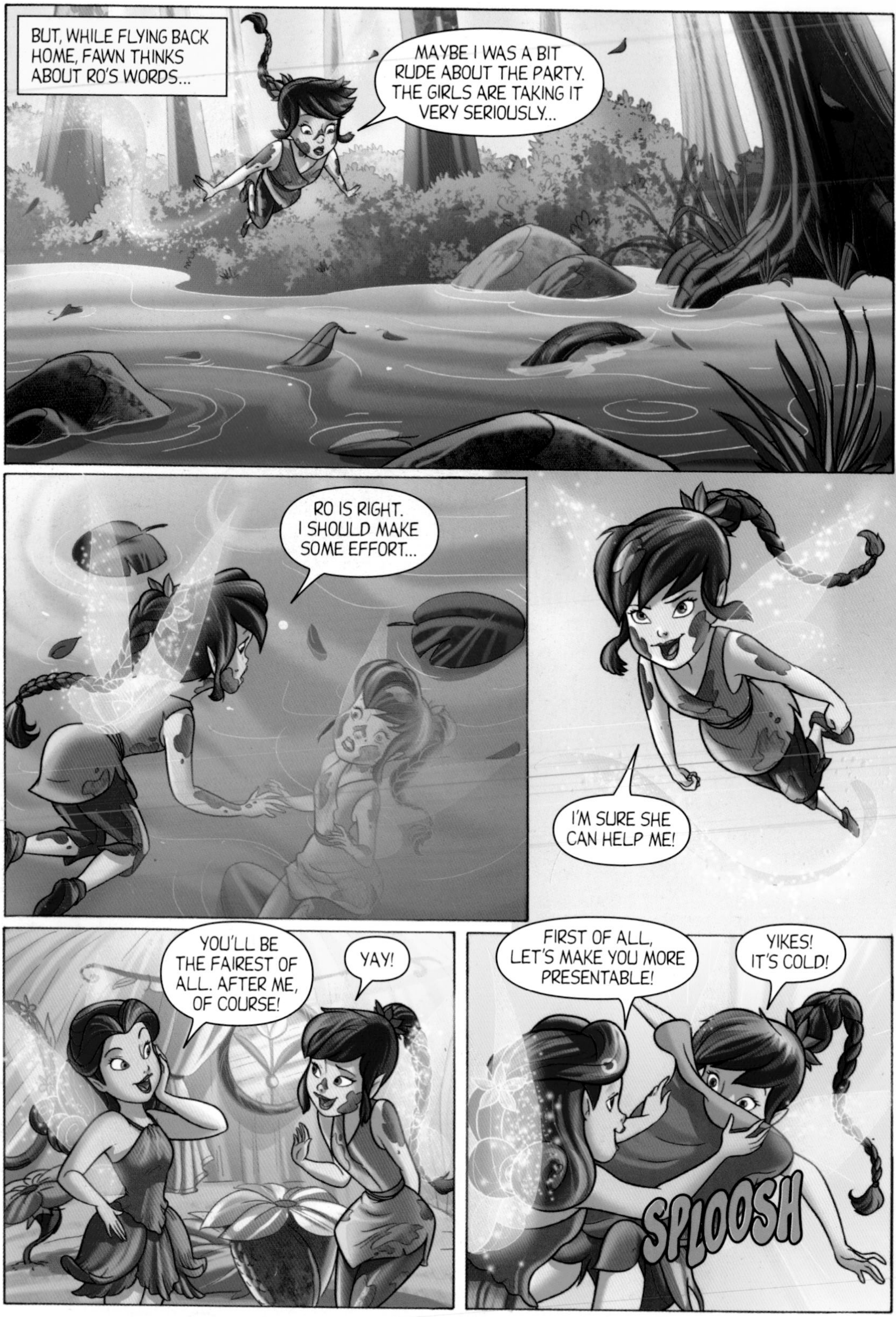
BUT, WHILE FLYING BACK HOME, FAWN THINKS ABOUT RO'S WORDS...
MAYBE I WAS A BIT RUDE ABOUT THE PARTY. THE GIRLS ARE TAKING IT VERY SERIOUSLY...
RO IS RIGHT. I SHOULD MAKE SOME EFFORT...
I'M SURE SHE CAN HELP ME!
YOU'LL BE THE FAIREST OF ALL. AFTER ME, OF COURSE!
YAY!
FIRST OF ALL, LET'S MAKE YOU MORE PRESENTABLE!
YIKES! IT'S COLD!
SPLOOSH

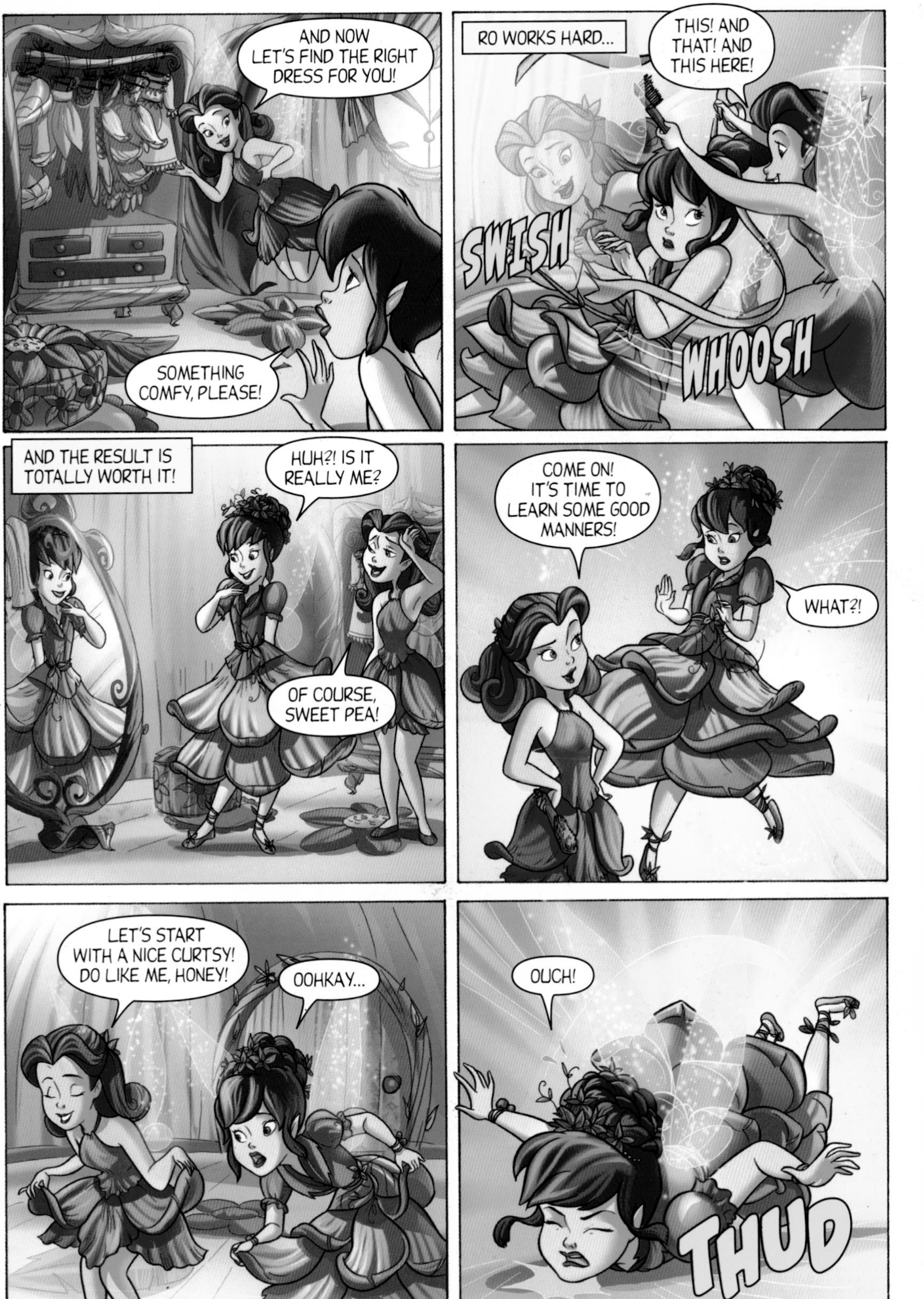
AND NOW LET'S FIND THE RIGHT DRESS FOR YOU!
SOMETHING COMFY, PLEASE!
RO WORKS HARD...
THIS! AND THAT! AND THIS HERE!
SWISH
WHOOSH
AND THE RESULT IS TOTALLY WORTH IT!
HUH?! IS IT REALLY ME?
OF COURSE, SWEET PEA!
COME ON! IT'S TIME TO LEARN SOME GOOD MANNERS!
WHAT?!
LET'S START WITH A NICE CURTSY! DO LIKE ME, HONEY!
OOHKAY...
OUCH!
THUD

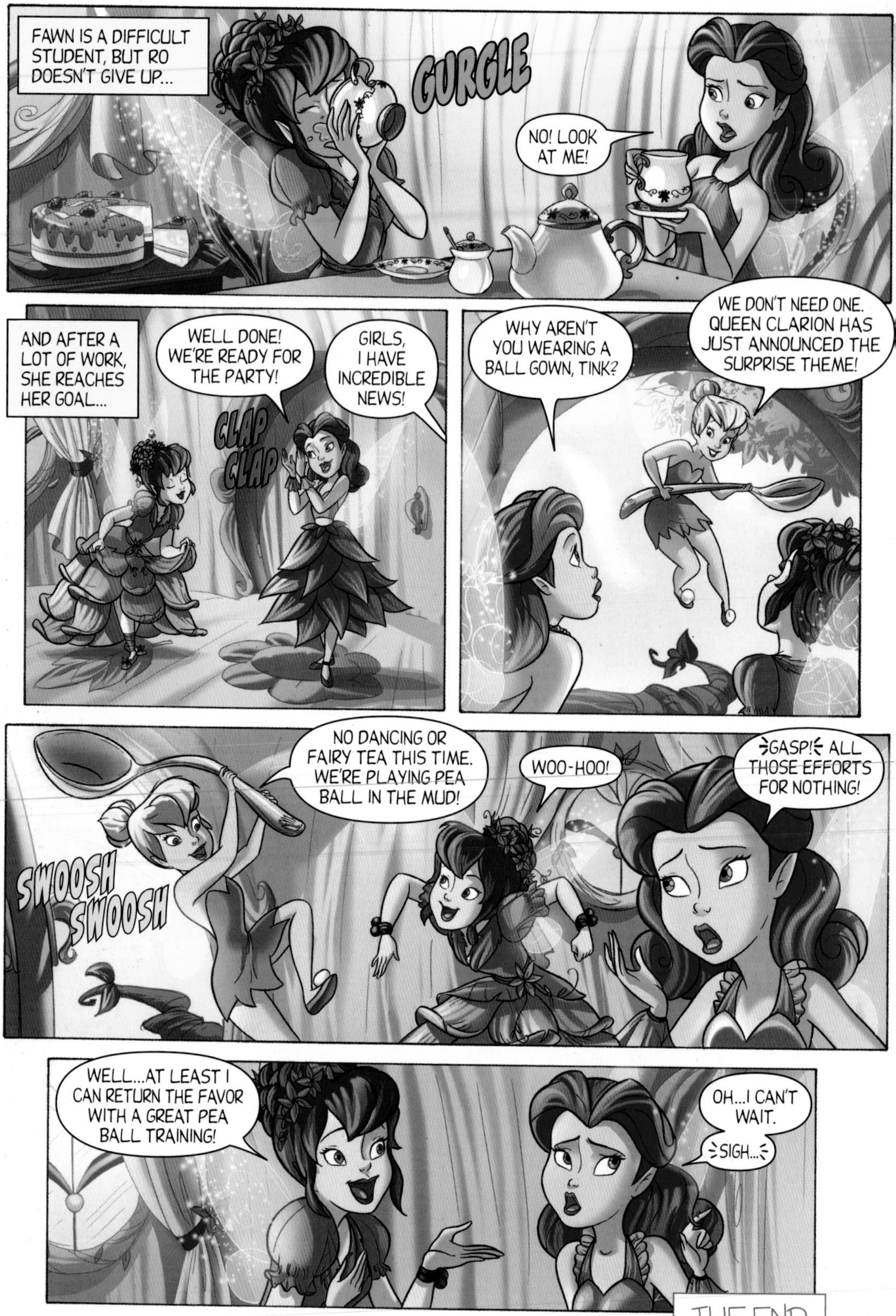
FAWN IS A DIFFICULT STUDENT, BUT RO DOESN'T GIVE UP...
GURGLE
NO! LOOK AT ME!
AND AFTER A LOT OF WORK, SHE REACHES HER GOAL...
WELL DONE! WE'RE READY FOR THE PARTY!
CLAP CLAP
GIRLS, I HAVE INCREDIBLE NEWS!
WHY AREN'T YOU WEARING A BALL GOWN, TINK?
WE DON'T NEED ONE. QUEEN CLARION HAS JUST ANNOUNCED THE SURPRISE THEME!
NO DANCING OR FAIRY TEA THIS TIME. WE'RE PLAYING PEA BALL IN THE MUD!
SWOOSH SWOOSH
WOO-HOO!
GASP! ALL THOSE EFFORTS FOR NOTHING!
WELL...AT LEAST I CAN RETURN THE FAVOR WITH A GREAT PEA BALL TRAINING!
OH...I CAN'T WAIT.
SIGH...
THE END

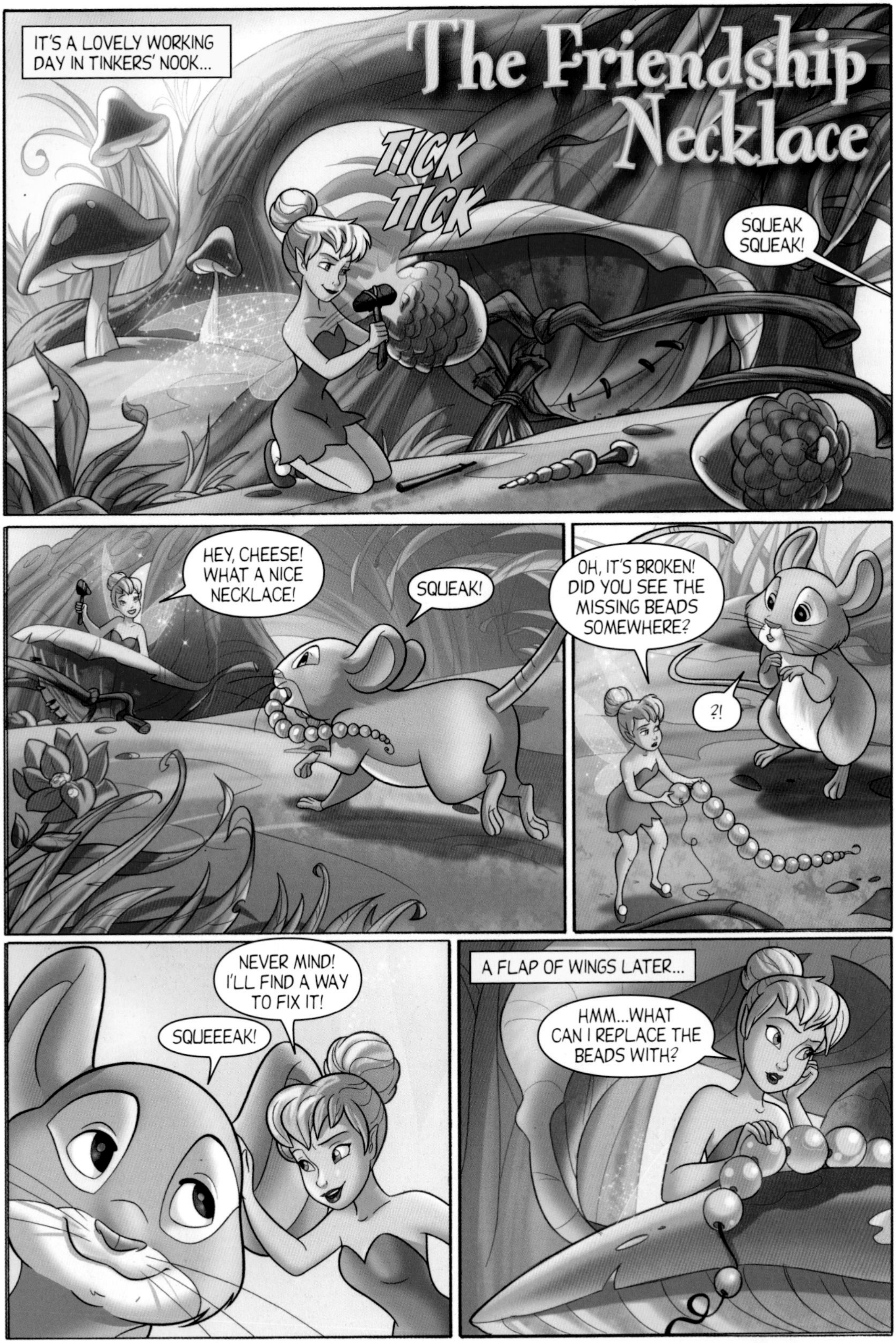

IT'S A LOVELY WORKING DAY IN TINKERS' NOOK...
The Friendship Necklace
TICK TICK
SQUEAK SQUEAK!
HEY, CHEESE! WHAT A NICE NECKLACE!
SQUEAK!
OH, IT'S BROKEN! DID YOU SEE THE MISSING BEADS SOMEWHERE?
?!
NEVER MIND! I'LL FIND A WAY TO FIX IT!
SQUEEEAK!
A FLAP OF WINGS LATER...
HMM...WHAT CAN I REPLACE THE BEADS WITH?

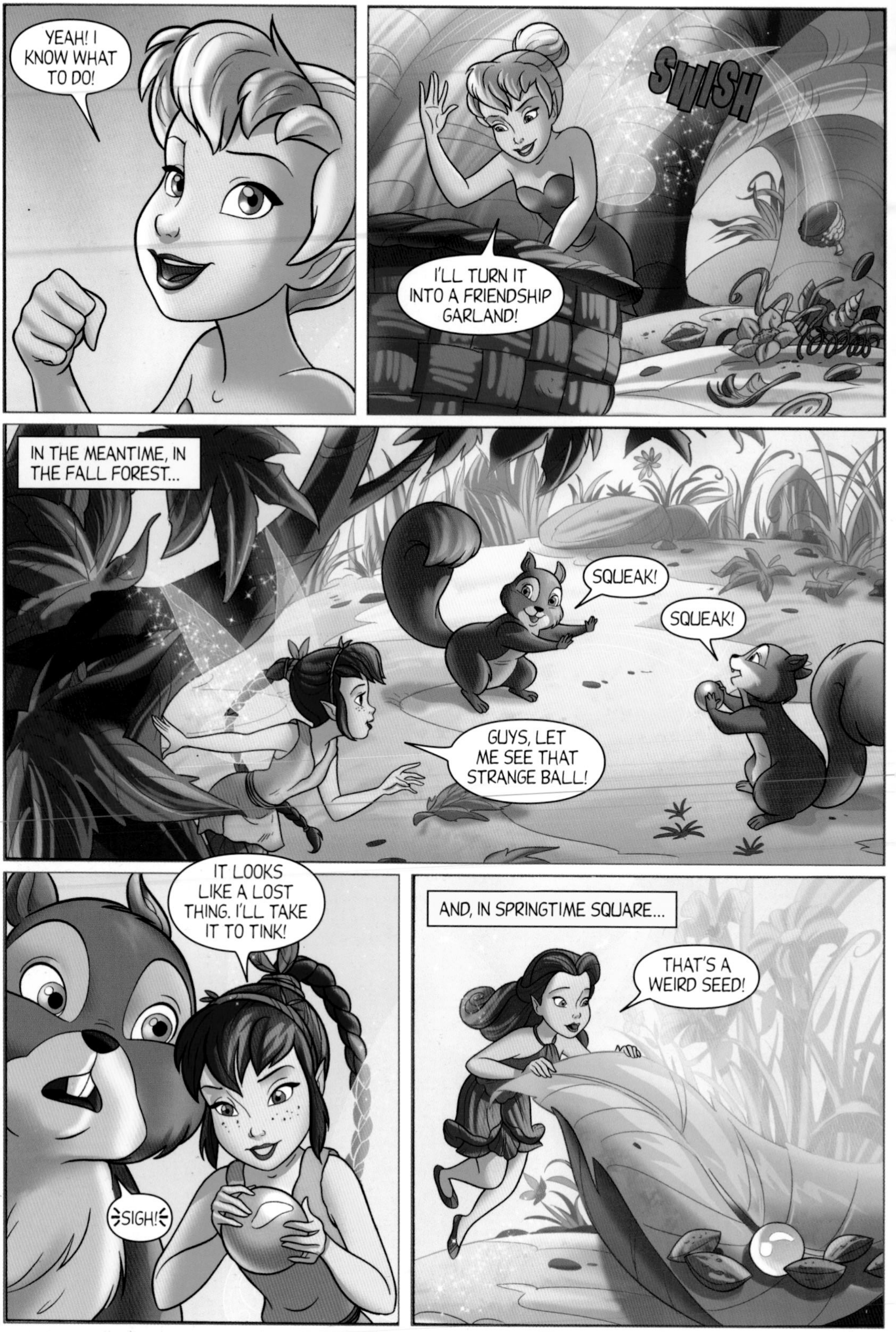
YEAH! I KNOW WHAT TO DO!
SWISH
I'LL TURN IT INTO A FRIENDSHIP GARLAND!
IN THE MEANTIME, IN THE FALL FOREST...
SQUEAK!
SQUEAK!
GUYS, LET ME SEE THAT STRANGE BALL!
IT LOOKS LIKE A LOST THING. I'LL TAKE IT TO TINK!
SIGH!
AND, IN SPRINGTIME SQUARE...
THAT'S A WEIRD SEED!

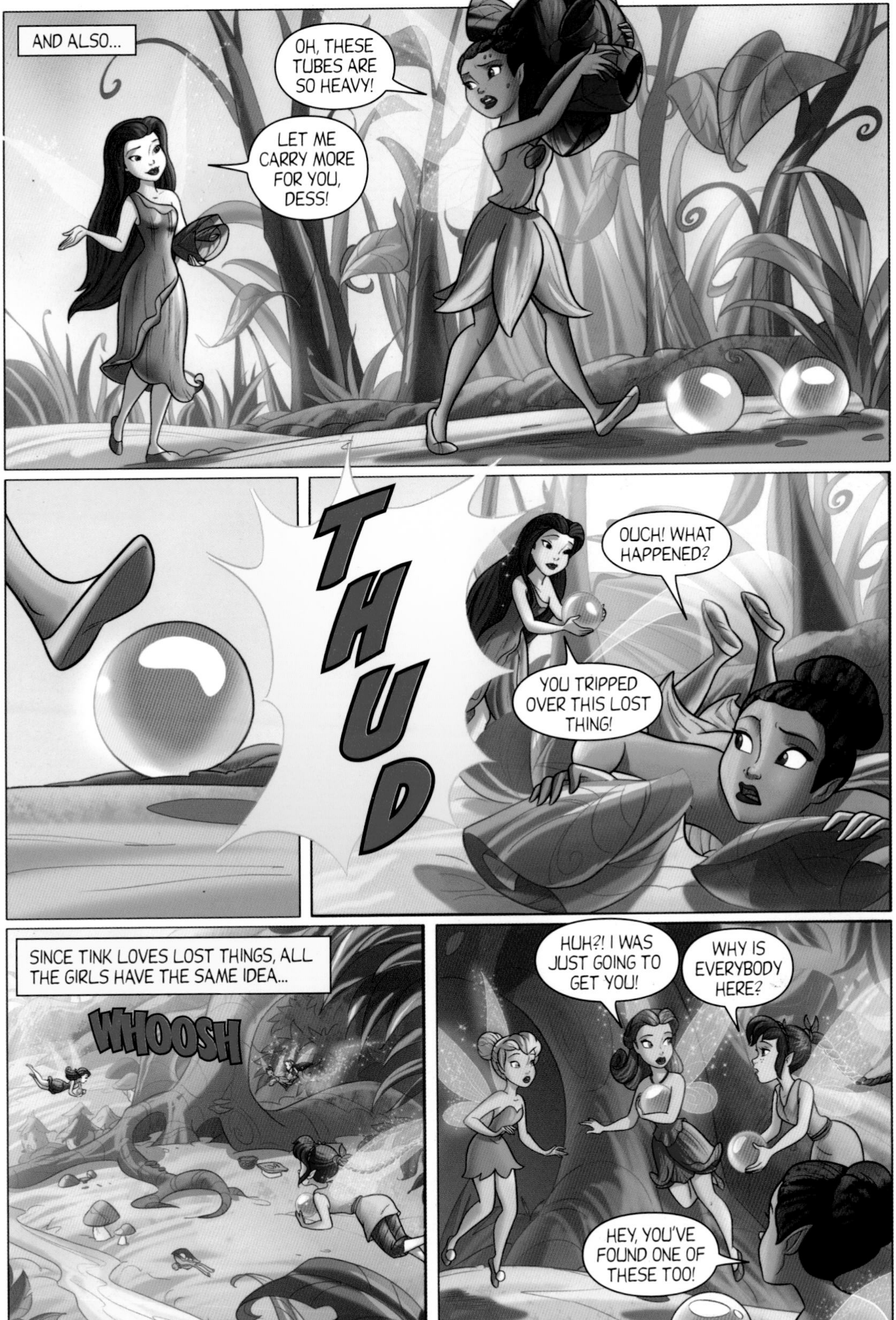
AND ALSO...
OH, THESE TUBES ARE SO HEAVY!
LET ME CARRY MORE FOR YOU, DESS!
THUD
OUCH! WHAT HAPPENED?
YOU TRIPPED OVER THIS LOST THING!
SINCE TINK LOVES LOST THINGS, ALL THE GIRLS HAVE THE SAME IDEA...
WHOOSH
HUH?! I WAS JUST GOING TO GET YOU!
WHY IS EVERYBODY HERE?
HEY, YOU'VE FOUND ONE OF THESE TOO!

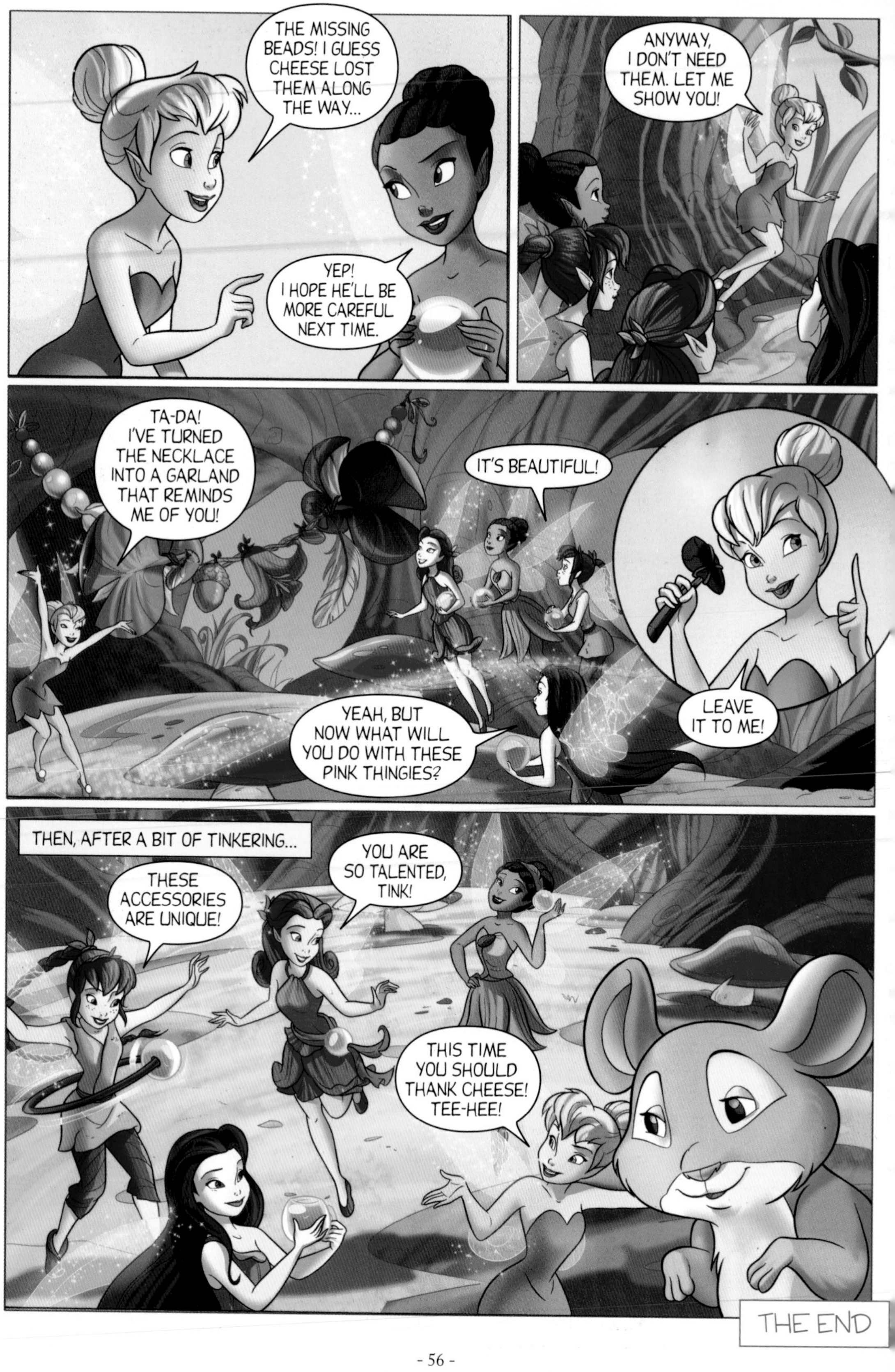
THE MISSING BEADS! I GUESS CHEESE LOST THEM ALONG THE WAY...
YEP! I HOPE HE'LL BE MORE CAREFUL NEXT TIME.
ANYWAY, I DON'T NEED THEM. LET ME SHOW YOU!
TA-DA! I'VE TURNED THE NECKLACE INTO A GARLAND THAT REMINDS ME OF YOU!
IT'S BEAUTIFUL!
YEAH, BUT NOW WHAT WILL YOU DO WITH THESE PINK THINGIES?
LEAVE IT TO ME!
THEN, AFTER A BIT OF TINKERING...
THESE ACCESSORIES ARE UNIQUE!
YOU ARE SO TALENTED, TINK!
THIS TIME YOU SHOULD THANK CHEESE! TEE-HEE!
THE END

WATCH OUT FOR PAPERCUT Z™

Welcome to the ever-engaging, enchanting eighteenth DISNEY FAIRIES graphic novel from Papercutz, those happy dwarves (who hardly ever whistle while they work) dedicated to publishing great graphic novels for all ages! I'm Jim Salicrup, the somewhat Sleepy Editor-in-Chief, and something of a combination of Doc and Dopey!

If this is your first DISNEY FAIRIES graphic novel, allow me to explain that you never know what you'll be getting from one DISNEY FAIRIES graphic novel to the next. This time around there's a dozen delightful stories featuring the denizens of Pixie Hollow. Sometimes there's just one big story—often based on one of the wonderful Tinker Bell DVDs. It's fun to mix things up and keep things fresh and exciting and full of surprises.

The big surprise this time around, aside from appearances by Nyx, Periwinkle, and even a brief flashback of Gruff, is a peek at an exciting new series featuring the one and only Mickey Mouse! Mickey is probably the ultimate Disney star, the one that has been there ever since the start of the Disney studio way back in 1923. In fact, Walt Disney himself said it best. When commenting on the success of Walt Disney Productions, he advised that we should never forget, "it all started with a mouse."

Mickey Mouse is so much more than just the iconic corporate symbol for Disney. He's been a star in everything from movies, TV, video games, and comicbooks. MICKEY MOUSE comics have been published all over the world in many languages. In Italy Mickey is known as Topolino, and his digest-sized comics magazine, *Topolino*, has been continuously published since 1949 (although there were even earlier *Topolino* comics prior to that). Mickey's comics are a lot of fun, and many of the stories created in Italy are now being published in the new MICKEY MOUSE comicbook from IDW. The Mickey Mouse series that we'll be publishing in our ongoing DISNEY GRAPHIC NOVELS series is called X-Mickey, and it features Mickey investigating various supernatural phenomena, starting out with what appears to be ghosts.

Personally, I've been waiting to enjoy these stories myself for some time, but unfortunately I don't understand Italian. One of the greatest benefits of being the Editor-in-Chief of Papercutz is that I'm often lucky enough to publish comics from other countries in English. So now, not only can I now enjoy X-Mickey, you can too. The first X-Mickey story appears in DISNEY GRAPHIC NOVELS #2, and we even have a special preview in a couple of pages right here.

Enjoy X-Mickey. Enjoy DISNEY FAIRIES. Most important of all, keep believing in "faith, trust, and pixie dust"!

Thanks,

Jim

STAY IN TOUCH!

EMAIL: salicrup@papercutz.com
WEB: papercutz.com
TWITTER: @papercutzgn
FACEBOOK: PAPERCUTZGRAPHICNOVELS
REGULAR MAIL: Papercutz, 160 Broadway, Suite 700, East Wing, New York, NY 10038

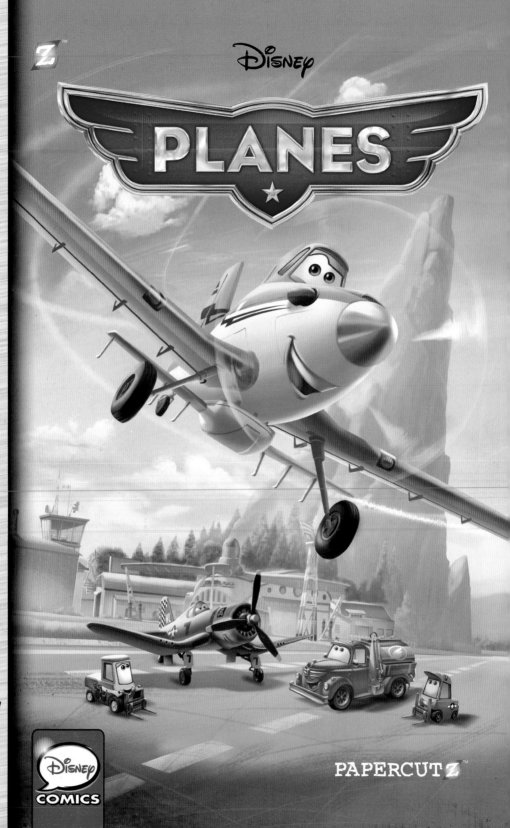

Special Preview of DISNEY GRAPHIC NOVELS #2 “X-Mickey”…

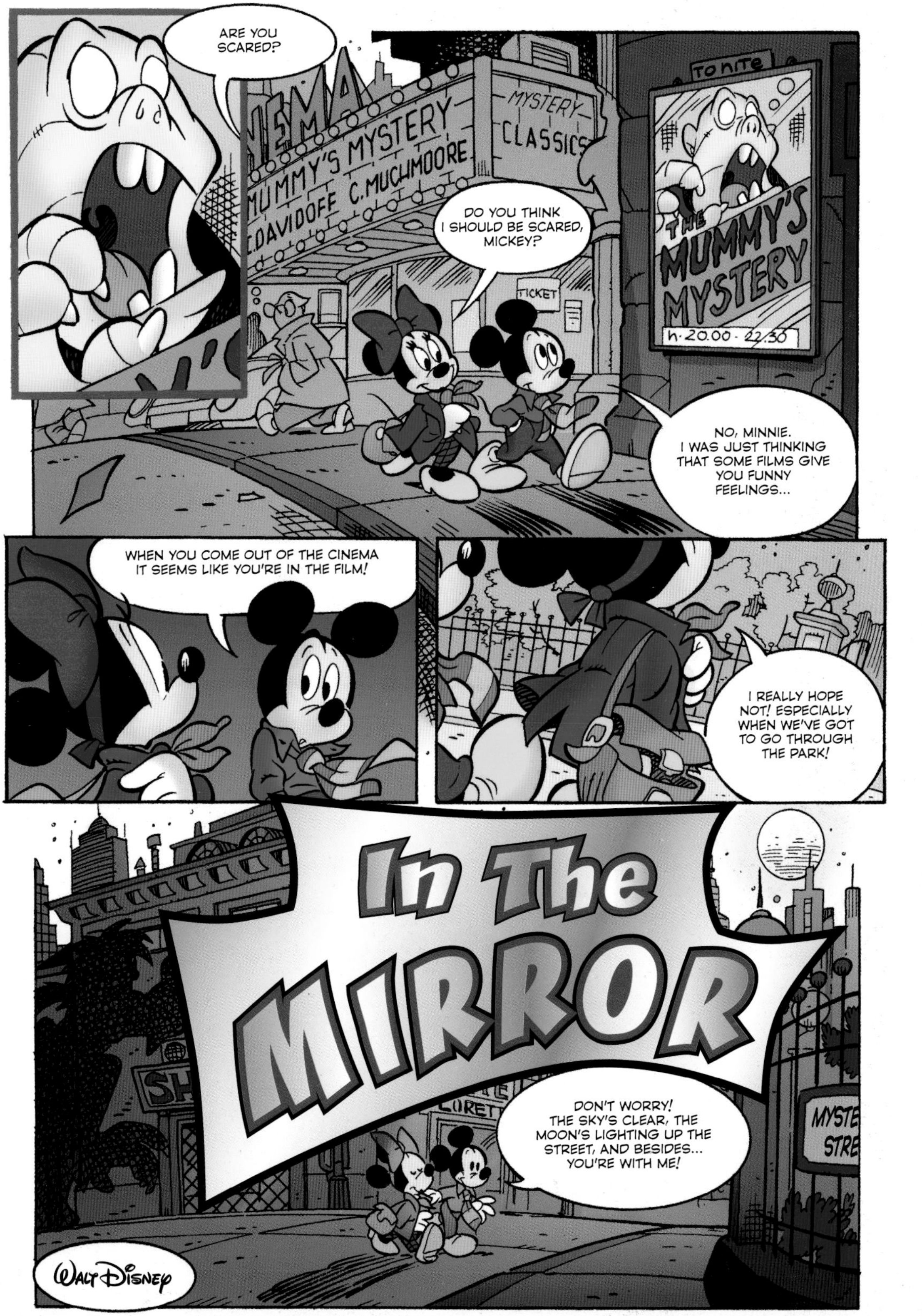
ARE YOU SCARED?
NEMA
MUMMY'S MYSTERY
C.DAVIDOFF C.MUCHMOORE
MYSTERY CLASSICS
TONITE
THE MUMMY'S MYSTERY
h. 20.00 - 22.30
TICKET
DO YOU THINK I SHOULD BE SCARED, MICKEY?
NO, MINNIE. I WAS JUST THINKING THAT SOME FILMS GIVE YOU FUNNY FEELINGS...
WHEN YOU COME OUT OF THE CINEMA IT SEEMS LIKE YOU'RE IN THE FILM!
I REALLY HOPE NOT! ESPECIALLY WHEN WE'VE GOT TO GO THROUGH THE PARK!
In The MIRROR
DON'T WORRY! THE SKY'S CLEAR, THE MOON'S LIGHTING UP THE STREET, AND BESIDES... YOU'RE WITH ME!
WALT DISNEY

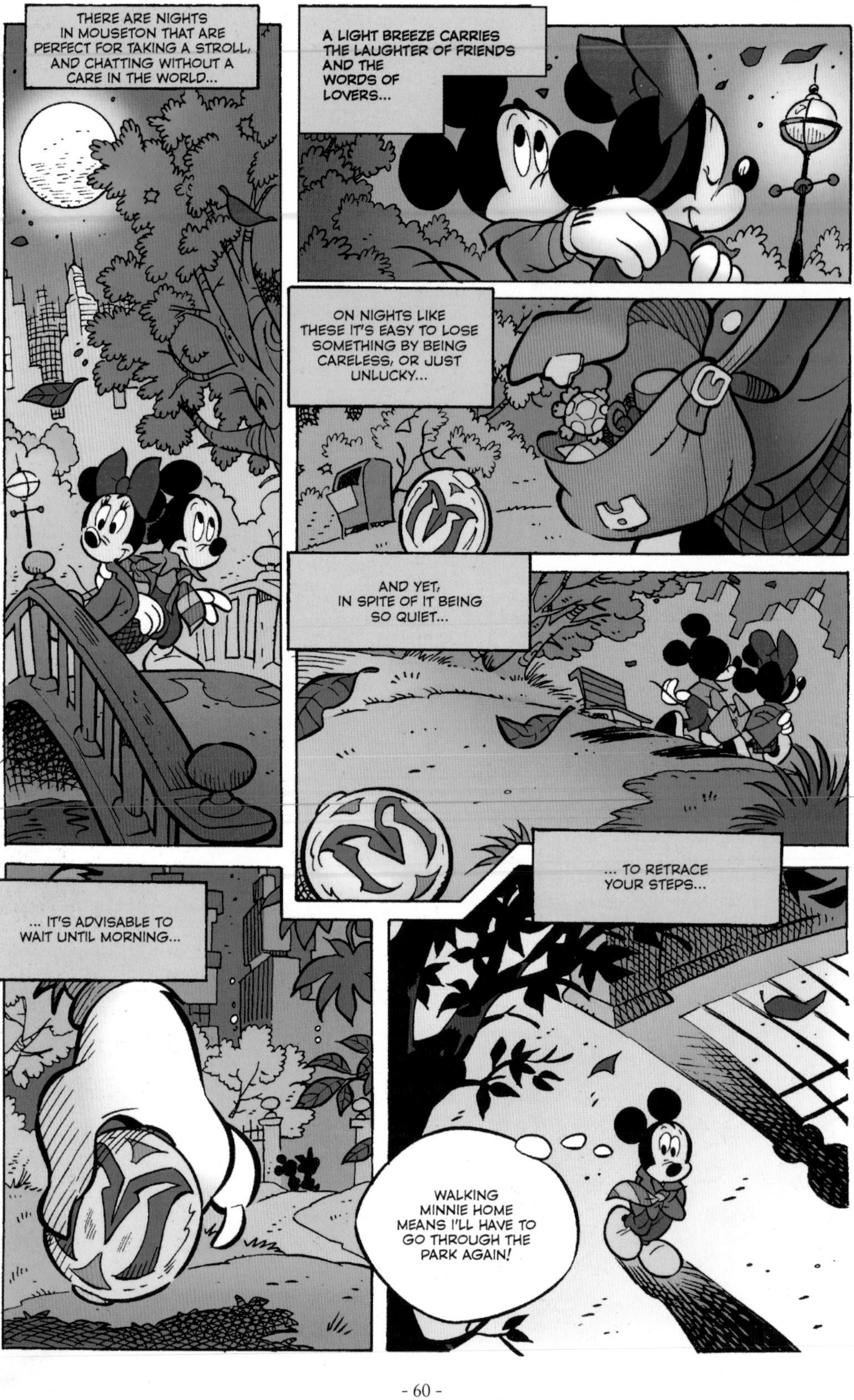
THERE ARE NIGHTS IN MOUSETON THAT ARE PERFECT FOR TAKING A STROLL, AND CHATTING WITHOUT A CARE IN THE WORLD...
A LIGHT BREEZE CARRIES THE LAUGHTER OF FRIENDS AND THE WORDS OF LOVERS...
ON NIGHTS LIKE THESE IT'S EASY TO LOSE SOMETHING BY BEING CARELESS, OR JUST UNLUCKY...
AND YET, IN SPITE OF IT BEING SO QUIET...
... IT'S ADVISABLE TO WAIT UNTIL MORNING...
... TO RETRACE YOUR STEPS...
WALKING MINNIE HOME MEANS I'LL HAVE TO GO THROUGH THE PARK AGAIN!

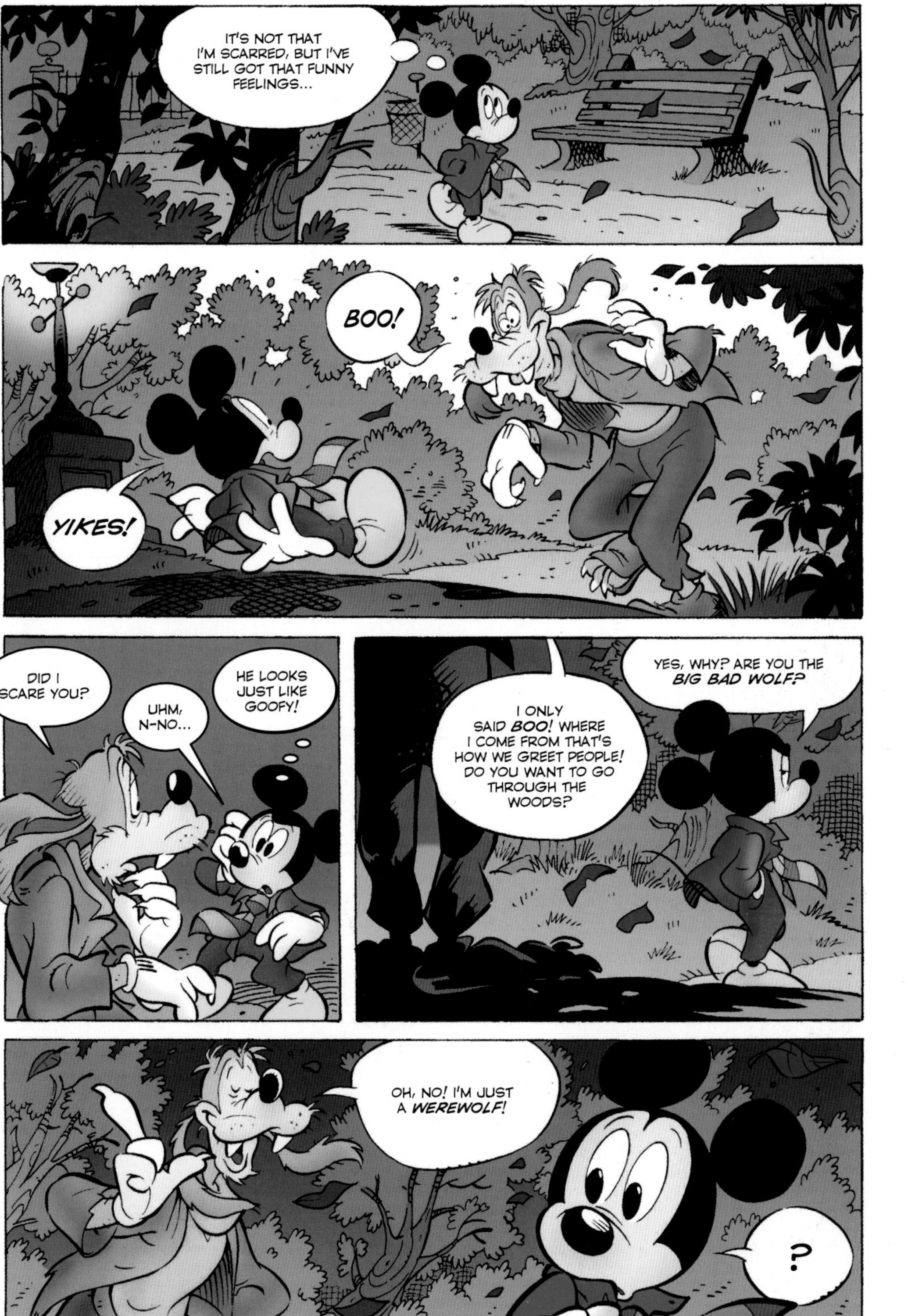

IT'S NOT THAT I'M SCARRED, BUT I'VE STILL GOT THAT FUNNY FEELINGS...
BOO!
YIKES!
DID I SCARE YOU?
UHM, N-NO...
HE LOOKS JUST LIKE GOOFY!
I ONLY SAID BOO! WHERE I COME FROM THAT'S HOW WE GREET PEOPLE! DO YOU WANT TO GO THROUGH THE WOODS?
YES, WHY? ARE YOU THE BIG BAD WOLF?
OH, NO! I'M JUST A WEREWOLF!
?

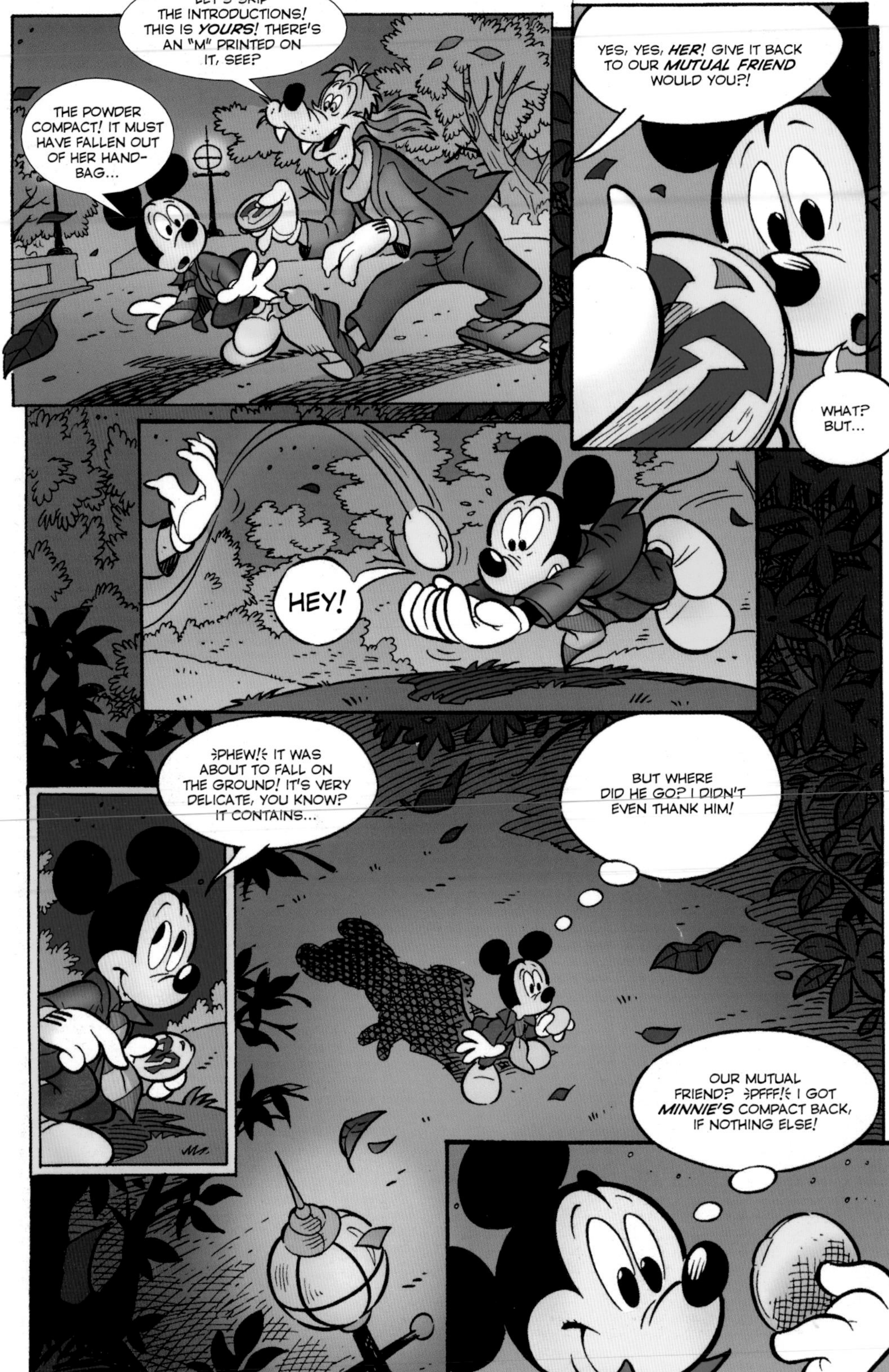
THE POWDER COMPACT! IT MUST HAVE FALLEN OUT OF HER HAND-BAG...
LET'S SKIP THE INTRODUCTIONS! THIS IS YOURS! THERE'S AN "M" PRINTED ON IT, SEE?
YES, YES, HER! GIVE IT BACK TO OUR MUTUAL FRIEND WOULD YOU?!
WHAT? BUT...
HEY!
PHEW! IT WAS ABOUT TO FALL ON THE GROUND! IT'S VERY DELICATE, YOU KNOW? IT CONTAINS...
BUT WHERE DID HE GO? I DIDN'T EVEN THANK HIM!
OUR MUTUAL FRIEND? PFFF! I GOT MINNIE'S COMPACT BACK, IF NOTHING ELSE!

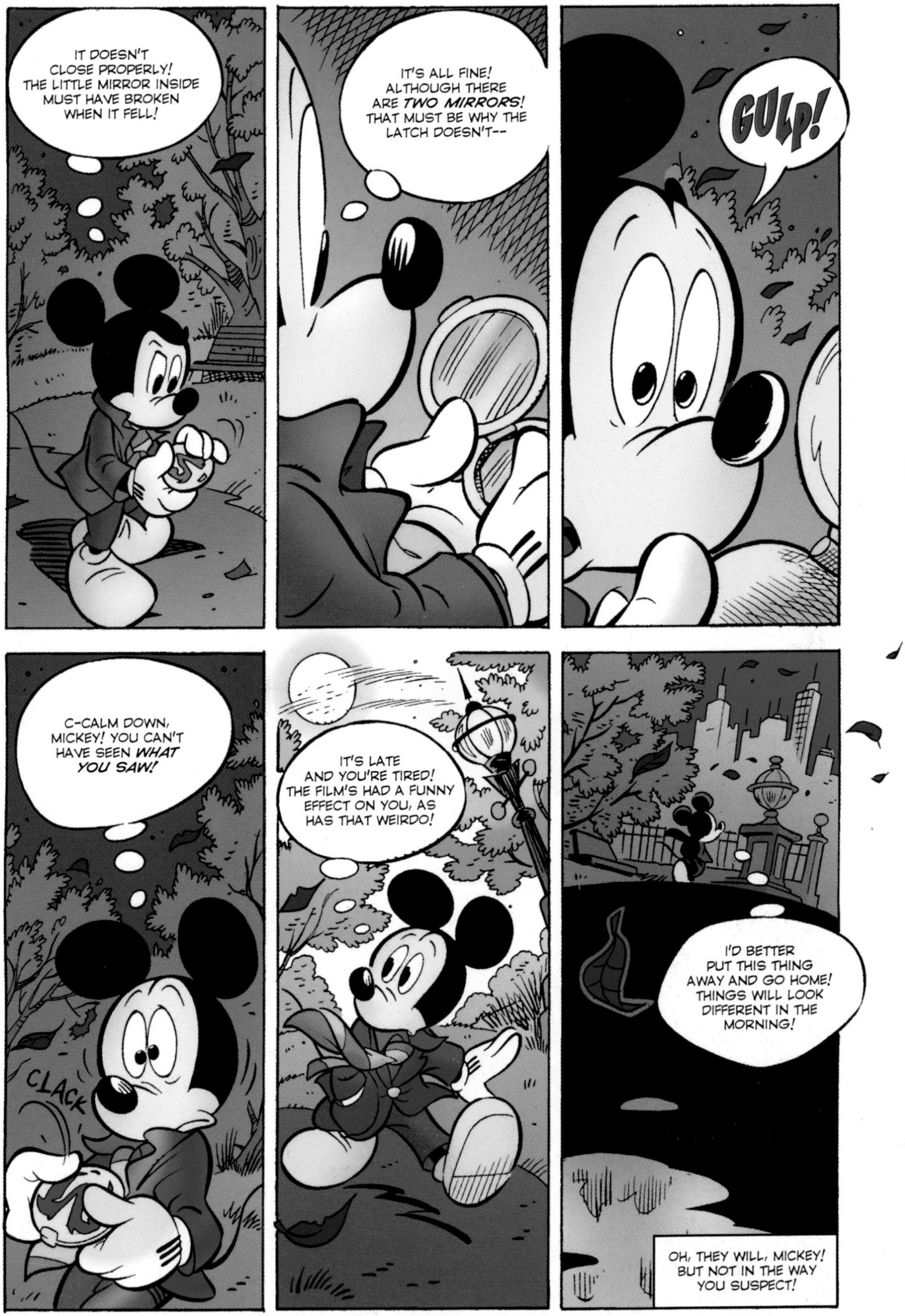
IT DOESN'T CLOSE PROPERLY! THE LITTLE MIRROR INSIDE MUST HAVE BROKEN WHEN IT FELL!
IT'S ALL FINE! ALTHOUGH THERE ARE *TWO MIRRORS!* THAT MUST BE WHY THE LATCH DOESN'T--
GULP!
C-CALM DOWN, MICKEY! YOU CAN'T HAVE SEEN *WHAT YOU SAW!*
CLACK
IT'S LATE AND YOU'RE TIRED! THE FILM'S HAD A FUNNY EFFECT ON YOU, AS HAS THAT WEIRDO!
I'D BETTER PUT THIS THING AWAY AND GO HOME! THINGS WILL LOOK DIFFERENT IN THE MORNING!
OH, THEY WILL, MICKEY! BUT NOT IN THE WAY YOU SUSPECT!

Don't miss DISNEY GRAPHIC NOVELS #2 "X-Mickey"—Coming Soon!

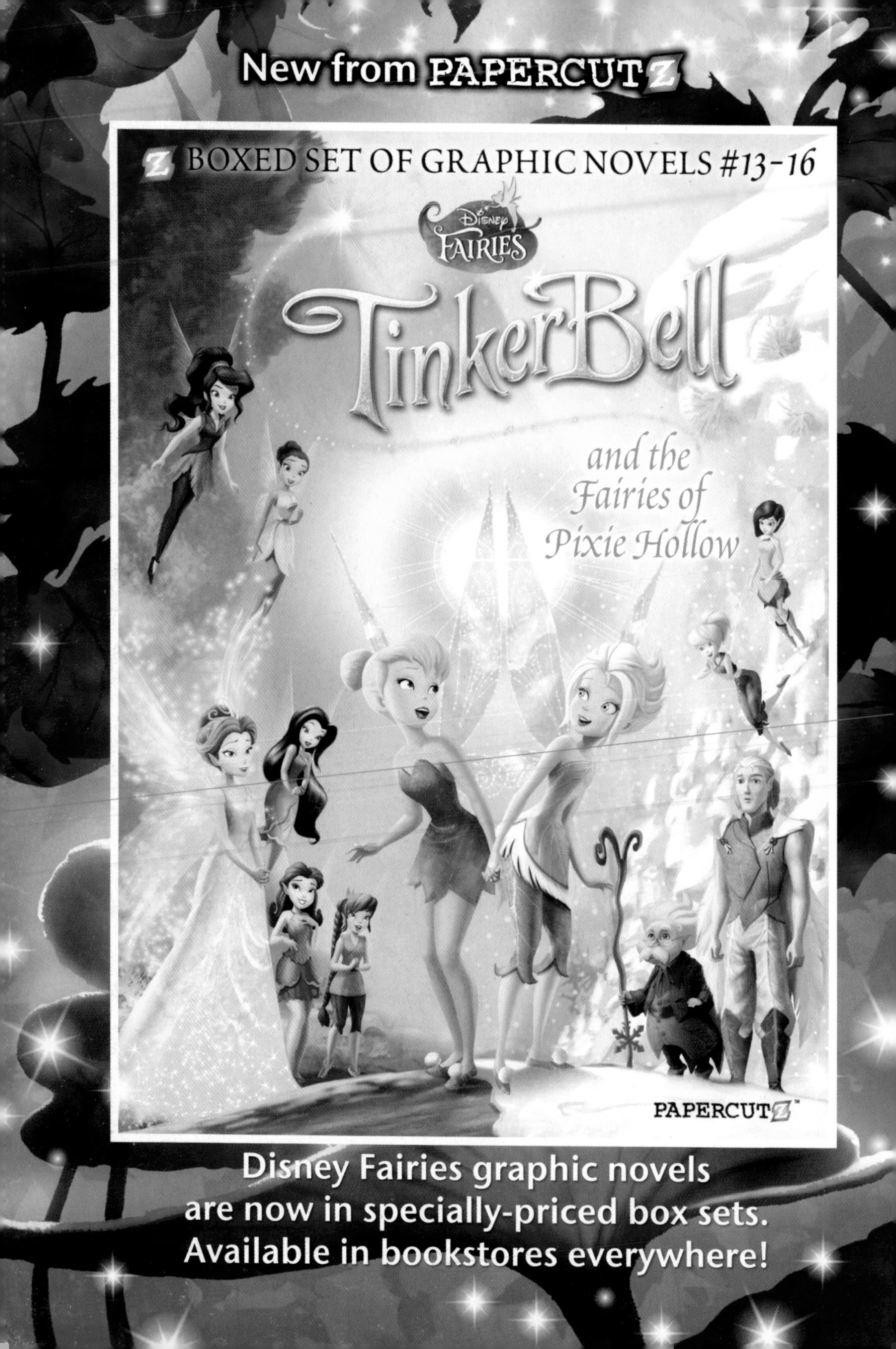
New from PAPERCUTZ
BOXED SET OF GRAPHIC NOVELS #13-16
Disney FAIRIES
TinkerBell
and the Fairies of Pixie Hollow
PAPERCUTZ
Disney Fairies graphic novels
are now in specially-priced box sets.
Available in bookstores everywhere!